A Howl in the Night

JK Brandon

ONE

As soon as I heard it, I knew something was terribly wrong.

It was long, low, and mournful, like a little hound heart was broken and nothing would ever make it right. A thousand hairs on my back stood straight up. Even Meatloaf woke up, and nothing wakes him up.

He thought it was the wind whistling through our wood-slat gate. It was the hot time, and sometimes dust storms blow in out of nowhere, like tonight. But I knew this was a different animal altogether.

I cocked my head like some mutts do when they don't get it, except I knew exactly what was up. Just then a big wind gust slammed the house, blowin' a bunch of seed pods out of our Mesquite tree and sending them raining down all over the patio.

That was it.

We bounced off the living room rug and bolted for the backyard. Pow! I blew the dog door at full speed, Meatloaf clippin' my heels. We stopped and went rigid out on the grass, straining to hear through the storm. The wind raised and rustled the long hairs of my black coat. I took a step forward and listened harder, desperate for a clue. Then it came again.

Wooooooooooooooooooooooooooooooooooooooooooooooooooooooo.

I shivered, even in the warm breeze.

It was Nelly, the little Beagle three-houses down. I'd heard her howl before, but not like this. Never. That's when I knew somethin' awful must have happened.

We looked helplessly at each other, there was nothing we could do, Nelly was three houses away. That's three yards with tall block fences and wood-slat gates as tight as a chain choke collar at full yank. Meatloaf let loose a couple of mean, rumbling barks, hoping to scare off whatever might be menacing the neighborhood. I did a quick perimeter check, ears up and nose to the ground. I nodded at my partner. The yard was clear.

Harley next door started with his baritone bark, then Roxie down the street, except her squeak wouldn't scare away a mouse. All around the neighborhood, dogs spoke up to warn the unwary—not at my house.

Meatloaf stood by my side. "Whadda ya think?"

I had my nose in the air, searching for tell-tale scents. "I don't like it. Smells like trouble comin' our way."

We ducked as a white light streaked past our house and flashed down the street, then streaked by once again.

Police-humans.

We dashed to the gate and stuck our noses through the slats. Best as I could smell, there was a lone female-cop at Nelly's place. Somebody must have called the police, probably that old busy-body across the street from us. She didn't sleep much, except during the day when we wanted to bark at cats.

Ghhetricmmspdpvkjfresjjttheehhsk.

A two-way cackled with cop talk in the night air, bouncing off the neighbor's house and funneling into our backyard. I knew a lot of human words, but I couldn't make any sense of this babble. No matter, I thought I knew what was up.

"Gotta be a burglary," I said.

Roxie was still barkin' on and off, and of course Harley the Rottweiler wouldn't shut up. Neither would that radio.

Kfjkfhjwurirnchdjdotiwmerhddhh.

We ran to the other side of the yard, but nothin' was shaking so we hustled back to our gate. I was gettin' nervous, the police shoulda been out of there by now. It was startin' to look bad for the Nelly household.

"Here comes another one," said Meatloaf.

There were two more, actually. Now we had three cop cars and two light bars strobing our street. It'd be different if this was Saturday night at the Deuce, but this was Scottsdale, baby. Nothin' bad ever happens up here.

"What about the police?" he asked.

I sniffed deep. "The female's still inside, but now there's four males out beatin' the bushes."

"Don't know, dawg, that's a lot of police for a burglary."

Meat was right. That many cops in one place usually meant a beer bust or a body turning cold. Even in this heat.

Then it hit me. The scent was faint, very faint—then all too strong. It floated over on the thick night-air when the wind died, invading my strongest sense. I stepped to one side and threw up. Meat couldn't smell it, but watching me retch, he knew what made me puke.

Blood.

"Woof Woof! Woof Woof!"

Meatloaf let 'em have it again. That started another round in the neighborhood, so I joined the chorus.

"Bow Wow Wow Wow!"

That felt great—until we got the word from the man.

Taser! Meatloaf! Get in here.

Busted.

Robert held the door open and waited for us. He had that face on.

No barking.

Heads hanging, we trudged back inside. I don't know if Robert heard the police but he didn't miss our warning. He told us again to shut it, then he turned out the light and went upstairs. It looked like the block party was over. Pretty soon it was as still and quiet as a pooch on the way to the vet.

Meatloaf plopped down on the carpet and went right out. He was snoring in no time, but I couldn't get poor Nelly out of my mind. Her sad howl reminded me of a bad affair and a hapless hound I've tried to forget. I put my chin on my paws and stared out into the darkness, thankful for my master and the roof over our heads.

When sleep finally came, my tired paws twitched and jerked to that same nightmare, that same horror, that same moment.

***

My eyes popped open at first light, but I lay there a while and analyzed the action at Nelly's. I tried to find a good side, but every way I flipped it, it came up trouble. Meatloaf and I know all about trouble, we been around the block before. We didn't just fall off the animal-control wagon.

By the way, we're Labs.

Black Labs.

Meatloaf was still sleeping, but I got up and stretched my legs. It seemed like it was brighter outside, which was a good thing, first-food would be coming up quick. I heard Robert moving around upstairs—heavy footsteps, water splashing, doors closing—stuff like that.

I was gettin' impatient, I wanted the day to get rolling. I'd have gone upstairs to see what the holdup was, but that's a big "No-No, Bad Dog" around here. But it was time to go, even Meatloaf started to stir from his spot on the carpet.

The noise upstairs got louder, so me and Meatloaf moved to the bottom of the stairs to whine and wait. When you're a dog, you spend most of your life waiting. Waiting for food. Waiting for pats. Waiting for a walk. If you're Meatloaf that's no problem, you just plop down and rest. Me, I gotta move.

So I left him huggin' the floor and went to see what was happening out front. I nosed the window shutter open and right away I spotted a rabbit sittin' in the yard. That just made me crazy, but I chilled. Those rabbits sit there like a statue and think we can't see 'em. Spottin's not the problem, catchin's the tough part.

I turned my head and saw a couple black and white cars down the street. At least that's the color I thought they were, because I got dog's eyes, and they stink during the day. According to the Animal Channel, we see shades of grey, washed-out yellows and blues—but no red or green.

A bark rumbled deep in my throat, but I choked it off. I didn't like these cop cars in my neighborhood, but I didn't want to make a fuss before we got something to eat. Sometimes you gotta stay focused.

Hi, guys!

It was Robert. He came down the stairs and rubbed our bellies while we rolled around on the floor like a couple of idiots. Robert went out to get the papers so I followed along to check things out. The rabbit outside was long gone, no surprise to me. The minute you get close to those long-eared rats they disappear like a dropped grape rolling by Meatloaf's nose.

Robert snagged the papers and glanced down the street at the black and whites. I wanted him to go check it out, but he went back inside to feed us, so I didn't wanna complain. I get a little nervous if I don't get my food first-thing, 'cause you never know if they're gonna forget you. Sometimes humans get their priorities screwed up.

So we got a couple cups of dry Eukanuba in separate bowls. I got the performance blend, Meat got the weight-control type. I don't much care for it; neither does my buddy, but he'll eat anything. I scarfed my chow down in a hurry so he couldn't steal any, then we hit the water dish for slurp and burp.

That's when the doorbell rang.

Normally we bark like crazy at the door bell, but I kinda expected this visit so I gave Meatloaf the look. I've seen these black and white cars before. I saw plenty of them during my time on the Westside; they bring cops in dark-gray uniforms with lots of questions. This morning I wanted to hear those questions.

7

I've learned a lot of human words in my time. It's not that unusual for a dog, not like a mutt opening a door or using a fork. I'm beyond all the normal words—eat, park, treat, stay—every hound knows those and more. Some dogs know a lot more, like me. You just gotta listen, these humans know some stuff.

We sat perfectly still in the living room so Robert wouldn't lock us up in the garage, but I put both ears up when they started talking. I picked out the human words I knew.

Good............Scottsdale.Police............hear............noise......
...killed.......neighbor............call.........anything...

Pretty soon I can't help it myself, I started pacing back and forth and whining.

Heeennnnnggg. Heeennnnnggg. Heeennnnnnnnnnnnnnnnnggg.

Robert pointed his finger at me.

Taser! Hush!

I needed to tell them about Nelly's howl last night, but they wouldn't listen to me. I don't get why they can't understand my words. I think it's a lip problem, their little human lips open and close real tight when their words come out. Me and Meatloaf, our lips don't close real good, they just kinda hang there, sloppy-like.

The cops finally left. Too bad, we didn't learn squat from that visit, it looked like we had to wait for dogs-at-dusk, our nightly mutt-meeting down at the park. If anyone knows what's goin' down around here, it's the neighborhood dogs.

TWO

Finally, Robert came home from work, but his mate didn't show her face.

I figured she was gonna be away a while longer, because Robert brought home a pizza for dinner. She's gone a lot, traveling for her job, whatever that is. She comes and goes with luggage bags that have really strange odors, weird stuff we've never smelled before. Stuff like different trees and different dirt and strange humans. Myself, I've never been to any of these strange places, but Meatloaf has. He's from California.

So Robert eats all his pizza and puts the box in the little plastic can in the pantry that ends up in the big recycle container. I looked at Meatloaf and he looked at me but we didn't let on nothin'. The plan was to come back late tonight when Robert was sleepin', and then we'd drag that pizza box through dog door and recycle it the Labrador way.

The bright day-light finally went down and it cooled off a little, so we stood by the kitchen drawer with our leashes in it and stared at Robert. He tried to ignore us, but we can out wait anyone. Eventually he gave in and hooked us up and out we went. Of course, Harley heard us leave and started barking. I think he was jealous.

Harley don't get out much, unless he breaks out. His humans keep him in the house at night because he barks at anything, even trees. So all night long it's: Woof Woof Woof. Woof Woof Woof.

What a loser.

On the way to the park we passed by Nelly's house, it looked different, not happy and cheerful like normal. The family cars were all gone and the house lights were out, and there was this yellow tape strung across the front door like ribbon on a rubber bone at Christmas time. Robert slowed up to look things over, and then we moved on to meet the pack at our little park to catch up on gossip and pee on the bushes.

There's always somethin' to talk about when we get together. At last night's meeting there was all this excitement about a coyote trottin' down the street, right through the middle of the neighborhood. Since the drought, food's been so scarce for 'em up in the foothills that they're coming down here and sneaking around, takin' our rabbits. Personally, I got no problem with less rabbits around here, but these bold coyotes are makin' some of our smaller mutts nervous.

Tonight the talk's gotta be the cop cars at Nelly's place.

When we got close to the park, Robert let us off the leash. I took off runnin' like a goosed Greyhound, but Meatloaf's got this gimp shoulder thing and he limps terrible when he runs, so I slowed down so he didn't look bad in front of the pack.

Most of the dogs were already there—sniffing the grass, doing their business or runnin' for exercise. Roxie was there, she's a cool Fox Terrier. She was chasing a Jack Russell named Gizmo. They're both just over a foot tall but they can run faster than a cup of bacon grease thru Meatloaf. Gizmo can jump five feet, straight up, even with those short little legs. Sucker can climb walls, too. But I was more interested in another dog. I was hoping to see the new pooch on the block, Simba.

I got lucky. She was there, looking sharper than I'd ever seen her.

If you didn't look at her face, you'd think she was only two. She was tight-bodied and slim, except for those long, powerful thighs. Her coat was thick, shiny and clean. She stood tall for a female Golden Retriever, twenty-two inches I'd say, with legs from here to Sedona. She was about sixty pounds--long, lean and lithe.

She had a brain to go with that body, you could see it in those eyes. Her eyes were deep-deep-gray. They seemed to look right through you.

Problem was, I was a little late gettin' to the party. Bandit, that weasel Weimaraner from down the street was already chattin' up the doll.

I sauntered up to the two of them.

"Evening Simba, you're looking good tonight."

She tilted her head, coyly.

I turned to Bandit. "So, the Vet find out anything about that nasty skin rash?"

He looked confused, but I was already sniffing him out. It pays to know the competition. It smelled to me like his human switched his food again, the stingy male probably buys whatever's on sale. And his human drives a German car, too.

We'll see how long Bandit's coat stays shiny eatin' that cheap food.

At first glance, Bandit looked pretty good with all those young Weimaraner muscles rippling under his silver-grey coat. He was about the same size and weight as me, but height and muscles aren't everything—I know all about those bodybuilder types.

Bandit put his nose to my butt, returning the inspection. I don't much like being sniffed by male dogs, even less by him.

"Lemme know if you see anything you like," I told him. He broke away.

I nodded at the rest of the group. "Hey dogs."

"You hear about Nelly?" Roxie asked.

"No. What's up with the cops last night?"

"Her human—the female—was murdered in her bed."

Catcrap. What I feared most had actually happened. Why'd it hafta be the nice human? Nelly's female used to stop us and give us treats when we walked by on our way to the park.

Simba looked like she was going to cry. "Nelly's so upset, she walked though blood on the bedroom floor and everything. It got on her coat!"

Blood. It made me wanna puke just thinking about it. I tried to think of Nelly instead. "How's she doing?"

11

"Not good, I heard her crying this morning. Some human friends took her to their home."

"You sure it's murder? Couldn't be suicide or something?"

"Didn't sound that way to me," said Roxie.

Gizmo bounced over. "Did ya tell 'em? A killing right here on the street."

"I knew it." It was Buffy, the prissy little Bichon Frise with the diamond-studded collar. "First we get Miss Nelly-No-Papers moving in, then we get coyotes immigrating to the neighborhood. These low-life animals ought to be illegal."

Meatloaf jerked his head around like somebody yanked his chain.

"Hey, put a muzzle on it, you pedigree puke. No one cares that you're a Registered Purebred. And as far as those coyotes, they were on this land before we moved here."

Buffy tossed her head. "Well. If you're not going to keep the riff-raff out, why bother to live in a gated community? I ask you, whose human got killed last night?"

Simba's tail tucked between her tall legs. "I thought I would be safe in a rich neighborhood."

I jumped in. "OK, hold on everyone, let me think."

I had to chew on this, I didn't like not knowing what went on practically next door.

I asked Nelly's neighbor. "So Roxie, what'd you hear last night?"

Roxie seemed troubled, unusual for the happy Fox Terrier. "I heard glass breaking, then a while later I heard Nelly howl. I stood on the picnic table and bounced, but I couldn't see anything." She hung her head and looked down at her front paws. "I guess I should have barked more."

"It's all right, there was nothing you could do. Me and Meatloaf heard her howl, but we couldn't get to her either. These block fences make it feel like you're locked in the pound."

Buffy sneered. "Pound? I wouldn't know anything about that. Why don't you tell us what it's like, mister ex-con. I heard you were a pound puppy."

Gizmo snuck his long Jack Russell snout under Buffy's chest and flipped her backwards like he was turning over a Frisbee. "Go home, puff ball."

She ran off in a huff.

Simba looked a little upset by that, but she didn't say anything to Gizmo.

"What about Nelly's male?" I asked.

"He wasn't home, he travels for work," Roxie said.

"Bad break."

"Get this," said Roxie. "I stood next to the fence listening when the police-humans were talking. They were looking for a knife, because they said her throat was cut. That's why I know it wasn't suicide."

We considered the weight of that until a newly-arrived dog offered his opinion.

"I wager a coyote snuck in the backyard and went through the dog door." It was Winston, the English Bulldog. Winston was about a foot tall and two-feet wide, with an imagination bigger than Meatloaf's appetite. "I bet the blagger crept down the hall to her bedroom and slashed her throat wide-open with his razor-sharp fangs."

"Oh my," said Simba.

"Cool," said Gizmo. "A serial killer coyote."

Winston ignored him. "They're a bad lot. Best to keep away from them, they'll kill us all before it's over."

I scratched behind my ear and tried to squelch the subject. "Yeah right, Winston. You eatin' the neighbor cat's food again?"

Meatloaf sniffed the air. "You know, I thought his butt smelled funny."

Winston looked defensive. "I'll have you know bears eat fish."

I asked Roxie another question. "You hear the police say anything else?"

13

She thought. "I heard a lot of police words, but I didn't understand much of that."

"How about earlier," I asked. "You hear anything in the house?"

"I must have heard something, because it woke me up. It was stuff moving around outside."

"In the front or back?"

"The back. It was like a scraping on the ground."

That didn't make any sense. "Scraping?"

"Like something scraping, dragging on the gravel yard."

"Before Nelly's howl?"

"Yeah."

"Before or after you heard the glass breaking?"

"Before. It was real faint, I could be wrong."

Bandit scoffed. "I didn't hear anything. You must have been dreaming."

I ignored the pushy Weimaraner and kept talking to Roxie. "You smell anything unusual?"'

"It was windy, remember? Any scent from her house got blown away from me. All I could smell was creosote bush coming off the desert."

I looked around the pack. "Anybody else got anything?"

Winston did.

"The male, what's his name?"

"Victor, and his mate's name was Vickie. Victor and Vickie, nice couple. Or they were."

"Yes, yes," Bruno said. "But they argued. I heard them yelling when I walked by. I go by every day with my humans."

Roxie disagreed. "No way. They're Italian, that's not arguing, that's just conversation."

I didn't know about that. "Anybody ever been over their house?"

Gizmo had.

"My humans were friends with Nelly's humans. We used to go over there for a barbeque and swim."

My humans did that sometimes, too. But they never took us, 'cause I guess two Labradors at a barbeque was asking for trouble.

"They were friendly," said Roxie.

"Vicki was friendly, but he yelled at me once for digging around his plants," Gizmo said.

That kind of yelling sounded normal to me, but a murder at a friend's house was anything but normal. It called for extra attention.

"I think everyone oughta keep an eye on their neighbor's place," I said.

"You mean bark more than normal if we hear something funny?" said Gizmo.

"Bark, run around, let 'em know you're watchin' the place. It won't hurt to be extra alert. We wouldn't want anything to happen to our masters."

"That's right," said Roxie. "I'm still jittery, it happened so close to me."

I felt sorry for her, it had to be a bad feeling. The murder could have been at her place. I thought a united front would make us all feel better, so I asked my rival for help.

"Bandit, you're on the other side, you should be on your toes, too."

He turned away and didn't say anything.

"Hey Bandit, you gonna help us or not?"

He weaseled, just like I expected.

"You know, they have police-humans for these kind of things," he said. "If we try to get involved, we could confuse matters."

"You think we should hide in our yards and hope we're not next?"

Bandit took two steps closer to me. "What I think, is you're making something out of nothing. This death was unfortunate, but Nelly will find new humans. There are plenty of humans out there."

His attitude got me hot under my dog collar. "That's it? Just get another sucker to fill your bowl?"

"Humans need us as much as we need them."

"So much for the love," Gizmo said.

Bandit sneered. "They'd dump us in two shakes if we didn't please them, so where's your love there?"

I didn't believe that for a moment. "Not my master, he cares about us."

"That's right," said Meatloaf.

I got right in Bandit's face. "I don't know about you, but I get a little worried when humans start gettin' killed in my neighborhood."

He shrugged. "If you want to worry about something, worry about the coyotes."

Simba nodded. "I'm worried about coyotes."

Coyotes weren't the worst threat to our neighborhood, but I didn't want to contradict Simba in front of everyone. Bandit was another deal.

"OK, Bandit. I guess you don't wanna help. Anyone else out?" I looked at each muzzle. Nobody moved but Bandit. He turned and scratched the ground with his hind legs, throwing grass in my direction, like he was through with us. Then he ran off.

When I glanced over at our humans, they were standing in their own huddle on the sidewalk. It wasn't like a normal night. Nobody was joking around, throwing a ball and nobody was smiling. They looked like they'd just stepped in dog vomit.

I turned to the pack. "OK, mutts. I think we got a problem here. We gotta stick together and take care of our homes."

They barked sharply and ran off.

***

When me and Meatloaf got back to the house, we flopped down on the cold tile and panted like crazy. After we cooled down a little, we drank two bowls of water, but then we dripped a bowl's worth back on the floor.

No problem, we never worry about water around here. Robert gives us fresh water twice a day. In case he forgets, there's always the big white water-dish in the bathroom, as long as the lid is up.

16

Robert turned the television on and flipped channels like he always did, but this time he stopped at one channel and turned the sound up. I wandered over to see if it was the Animal Channel, but it looked to me like a female news-human talking while holding a wire or something. I think she was standing in front of Nelly's house, because that same yellow tape was on the door and she was talking about murder in Scottsdale. Robert listened and I listened but I didn't understand all her words.

I did notice the female on the television had hair like a Golden Retriever and a chest like a Bulldog. She seems to be on a lot of the different channels.

We sprawled on the floor at Robert's feet and fell asleep while he watched more television. Sometime later he got up, turned off the TV and started turning off lights. That was our sign to stand by the pantry door and wait for a dog bone treat. Meatloaf scooped his up and ran off, but I left mine on the floor and stared until Robert put a second bone down. He winked at me and turned off the last light.

I put both bones in my mouth and snuck into the laundry room, then stopped and listened. All I heard was Robert's footsteps upstairs and Meatloaf chomping away in the living room. I snuck out the side dog-door and trotted to the metal view fence in the rear of the yard. It was hot and still, there was no nightlight shining yet.

I put the bones between the metal fence bars and ran back on the patio to sit and wait. Some time went by, not too much. Finally I saw two tiny glowing dots out in the desert. They seemed to dance and float, but grew larger every second.

"What the heck you doing?"

"Shhhhhhh! You scared the catcrap outta me, Meat."

"What're you doing out here? I thought we were gonna get the pizza box."

"Shhh. Lie down and wait. And no barking."

We put our chins down on the patio. The glowing dots bounced closer and closer to our fence. I could feel Meatloaf trembling, so I nudged him to keep him quiet.

Finally, an incredibly-thin body appeared, trotting thru the desert night on four long, skinny legs. It seemed so thin and top heavy I was afraid it might just fall over in a breeze. The ghostly form came right up to our fence and took the dog bones in its mouth. It turned to go, then paused and looked back at the two black bodies crouched on the patio. The pair of yellow eyes narrowed.

Then the shape vanished.

"Taser! What're you doing?"

"I gave it my bones."

"Are you crazy? That's a coyote."

"It's a mother," I said. "You can see her teats are swollen."

"If our pack knew this they'd go nuts. A coyote!"

"She's starving," I said.

"Yeah, well, we can't be feeding everyone in the neighborhood."

Meatloaf was right, of course. But I hadn't been able to get that desperate skeleton out of my mind since she showed up at our fence days ago.

"No, buddy, we can't feed everyone. But we can feed this one."

I knew somewhere out there was her litter, a few tiny pups that would never get enough to eat, even if they survived the blazing summer.

We lay side-by-side on the patio, staring far out into the night, listening to faint coyote howls echo off the desert hills. A long time passed, but we never moved.

Somehow, we'd lost our appetite for the pizza box.

THREE

Four years previous, Westside Phoenix.

I put my paws on the front window and my nose on the glass. It's dark both outside and inside now and my human still isn't home.

The houses on our street all have a car or truck in the driveway and some lights on in their windows. I can see the neighbor humans walkin' around talkin' and stuff. Some of them are sittin' out front on lawn chairs, drinking beer out of those cans. The human across the street takes a long drink and throws his can at a cat sitting on his dirt yard, so it jumps up and runs away real quick. The humans laughed and got up and got another beer.

I think it was beer, 'cause sometimes my human gives me some when he drinks his beer. I don't really like the smell but the taste is all right. Most of the time I'd rather have some puppy chow, especially right now 'cause I haven't had first meal or second meal or any scraps today. My stomach hurts so I'd settle for anything. If we don't have dog food in the house, I get whatever my human doesn't eat for his dinner, and that tastes great, except sometimes it makes me throw up.

I get down from the window and walk in little circles, whining a bit. I'm a little worried he might not come home at all, like some nights. I lie down and try to sleep some more so I don't have to think about my stomach.

Next time I wake up it's darker in the neighborhood and I don't see many lights in the neighbor's windows any more. I go out in our backyard through the hole cut in the back door and walk all around our wood fence, sniffing a little, whining a little. Then I sit and scratch my ear with my hind leg 'cause it hurts and itches at the same time, but soon it feels a little better after all the scratching.

That's when I hear his truck pull in. I go back inside the kitchen and wait, my tail waggin' and my stomach growlin'. But he's just sittin' in the truck, not moving at all. Finally I hear the truck door open and hear him coming up to the front door, one hand dragging across the wall as he walks. Finally, he opens the door. He walks in kinda slow and stops in the middle of the room and calls out my name.

MAX!

So I run up to greet him but he kicks at me hard and yells something loud and mean and I know there's not gonna be a first-meal or a second-meal or anything else today. I run out to the back yard and sit shaking by the stinky garbage can. I wait a long time, until all the lights in the house are out, then I go to the back corner of the yard and go behind the dead bushes. The dirt is kinda damp there and the diggin' is pretty easy. It only takes me a little time 'cause I'd already dug out a spot to lay in. I dig fast with my front paws and the dirt flies back and hits the bush and pretty soon I'm under the fence and out the other side.

I shake off some dirt and start trottin' down our little street. I know I'm not supposed to be out, but now I don't care, I'm not goin' back to that place. I can make it on my own without humans. All I need to do is find some food and water.

I don't know too many dogs around here, because I don't get out of the yard much. About the only dog I know well is Cody. He's part Yellow Lab and part somethin' else, and he's a great friend, even though he's younger than me. Cody's skinny 'cause he's still pretty much a puppy but he's grown nearly full size. He comes by my fence a lot and we bark and play. There's not too-many dogs on a leash around here, mostly we just run around when we're out. It's kinda wild but I like it.

So this time I go by Cody's house. He's in the backyard but we don't bark, 'cause it's dark-time and we get in trouble if we bark too much then. We touch noses a lot and run back and forth, then I start digging under his wood fence 'cause I seen how easy it was at my place. He starts digging too, and pretty soon we're both out on the street, feelin' pretty tough, like a couple alpha dogs headin' a pack.

We cruise around the neighborhood for a while, then we stop at a dog's house that Cody knows. The Beagle isn't there or she's inside asleep, so we keep walkin' and lookin' for food on the sidewalk or in the yards.

Then we get lucky. I knock over a garbage can at some house without a fence and we eat what's left of a bag of bread. It tastes kinda sour but it feels real good to get somethin' in my stomach. So then we start trotting again. The lights on the street are mostly all out, and after a while we come to more streets all coming together and more cars and trucks driving by. I look at Cody and he looks at me, and I'm feeling not sure what to do next.

So we sit down on the sidewalk, panting and watching the cars and I'm thinkin' a drink of water would be good, but I don't see any puddles around here. I start to get up and look for some, but now I see a pickup truck pull up and stop across and down the street a bit. The truck headlights are on and the motor's running, but it's just sittin' there.

Then the door opens and this big dog gets out and stands next to the truck and stares at us. He looks like some bulldogs I've seen, but he's bigger and meaner looking, with short pointed ears sticking straight up. He's got muscles everywhere, and he looks like he weighs as much as me and Cody put together. His coat is all dark except for a white patch on his chest that looks like a star. His snout is black, really black. His eyes look black too. The eyes are creepy, they never look anywhere but at us.

He stands frozen, staring at me and Cody, like he's waiting for something. The truck motor is still runnin' and the lights are still on.

Then I heard the human in the truck yell.

ZEUS!

KILL!

The dog leaps forward and runs right at us, full speed. I stand up and brace myself 'cause I'm not sure what's happening, but I know for sure who the alpha dog is now. I back up a little but Cody rolls on his back, puts his paws in the air and submits completely.

That's when this thing takes Cody's throat.

It opens its huge mouth and bites down hard, and all Cody can do is shake and kick and gurgle, but this thing bites harder and deeper and harder and deeper, and pretty soon Cody's legs aren't kicking anymore. I see his eyes, they're lookin' right at me, but—

I run.

I run like I've never run before. I run down the street for a long block and then in between two houses but now I gotta see. I'm panting crazy and my heart is pounding but I hafta stick my nose out and see. Cody's just lying there with the big dog standing over him. He's not biting Cody's neck anymore; he's just standing with his head up, looking down the street at the house where I'm hiding.

Then the human in the truck yells again.

ZEUS!

COME.

Zeus turns around and trots back to the pickup truck and jumps in. The door closes behind him. Then the truck just drives away.

I hide there, terrified, wanting my heart to stop beating so fast. But I get up and go back up the street to be with Cody. As I get closer I see he's not movin' at all.

I nudge him with my nose. He's all soft and rubbery, and somehow I know he's not my best buddy anymore. There's blood all over his neck and running down his fur and dripping on the street. I'm scared the truck will come back but I can't leave Cody again, so I stay and stare at the blood, even as this horrible smell tells me to run away.

I should have fought back.

The smell fills my nose.

But I didn't.

Wooooooooooooooooooooooooooooooooooooooooooooooooooooooo oooo.

FOUR

I stretched out on the grass and let the morning day-light warm my coat. I was cold from being inside under the airconditioning. It wasn't too hot outside yet, so me and Meatloaf soaked up some rays, rolled on our backs and got all filthy.

After a while I got hot and went inside. Like he did sometimes, Robert left the television turned on to keep us company, because he didn't want us to get lonely while he was at work. It was tuned to the Animal Channel, but I got bored with that and put my paw on the changer and flipped channels awhile. I saw that female-human with the Bulldog chest was on again.

After a few times around the channels I gave up 'cause I didn't find anything better. I didn't expect too, 'cause daytime television usually stinks. The History Channel looked promising for a while, but the commercials were too long.

So I went looking for something to eat. I can eat anytime, but I like to stay in shape. I'm about eighty-five pounds and a lot of that is muscle. I'm not sure what Meatloaf weighs, but he's heavier than me. Way heavier. I hear the Vet-human lecturing Robert when we go for a weigh-in, checkup, and the cold tube up your butt routine. I hate that part. Sure, they give you doggie biscuits afterwards, but it's not worth the violation to me. Taser don't take it in the rear for biscuits.

Meatloaf, he don't seem to mind.

Meat's almost seven. He's had different humans, same as me. His last was a female, but like the others, it didn't work out. He was already on thin ice for his propensity to pee wherever he wanted. Then

23

one day he ate her favorite pair of panties and shazam, he was down the road. Her friend at work, Robert, took him home.

Myself, I'm five. I'm no cherry, I did some hard time in the pound and I got the scars to prove it. I won't bore you with the depressing details, but trust me, it was no way to treat a Labrador. Then one day Robert walked in there and yanked me out of stir like a cactus needle from a sore paw. So I know when I got it good, I don't munch the furniture and I don't mess the carpet.

I didn't find any crumbs on the kitchen floor or the pantry, so I did some exploring and digging outside. I guess I was restless. I sniffed inside our plastic dog house, checkin' it for critters. I didn't find any 'cause Robert put it up on blocks to keep the crawly things out. Nothin' like a rattlesnake in your dog house to ruin your day.

Now it was really hot out, so I came back in to sleep in front of the TV.

I like having television-humans talking in the background. It calms me down and I learn interesting stuff and new words. But when I woke up later, the TV show was some dumb cat movie I couldn't get into. I wandered into the living room. Meatloaf was there, chillin' on the carpet. He watches a little television himself, mostly the Food Channel. I flopped down next to him on the carpet.

So there we were again, waiting.

I was still upset about the Nelly murder business, so I racked my brain trying to figure out what happened at her house. I thought I needed a better perspective on things. I eyed the staircase and made my decision.

"Hey, Meat. Keep an ear up for our humans, I'm going upstairs."

Meatloaf lifted his head off the floor. "Don't do it man, that's a dog felony. Last time you went up there they locked us both up."

I was already halfway up. "Sorry, buddy. It can't be helped. Bark if anyone comes home."

"Don't chew nothin'," he yelled after me.

I went in the master bedroom first, it had a wall of windows that looked out to the McDowell Mountains. It was a million-bone view of beautiful, flat desert rising up to low foothills. I saw our backyard perfectly and a little of the neighbor's yard on either side, but nothin' of Nelly's place from this room.

I did a quick inspection of the bathroom. There were some yummy looking Q-tips in the trash can, but I thought better of it. I sniffed the dirty clothes basket and some sweaty shoes in the closet. Then I looked higher. My female-human's sink counter looked spotless, while Robert's had all this stuff piled up on it, but I didn't have time to inspect it for chewables.

I padded over to the smaller room to the south. This was where Robert worked on his stuff, he calls it the hobby room. He builds these cool model airplanes out of light wood and thin paper, but they're not too strong. Me and Meatloaf can chew an airplane into a million pieces in the time it takes him to go poop in the bathroom. But that's another No-No, Bad Dog story.

I looked out the side window. I saw the house next to us with Harley the Rottweiler, then next to him was Roxie's house, then next to that was Nelly's. On the other side of her was Bandit's house. All our houses were in a row along the desert, it was kinda neat 'cause it's so close to the natural desert.

I concentrated on Nelly's backyard three houses down. It seemed normal to me. They had a swimming pool but they didn't have any grass in the back, just plants and trees and that crushed granite rock. Personally, I think it's uncomfortable to poop on. I'll take the grass any day.

But Victor had more trees than we did, and a lot of nice plants. He was always planting things and fussing in his yard. The guy had the nicest front lawn in our neighborhood, Robert says that's why none of the males like him. His lawn reminded me of the time me and Meatloaf stole those little white balls at that giant grass field we ran on, when some angry guys with sticks chased after us. But that's another No-No, Bad Dog story.

Victor didn't want us dogs on his grass either. If you happened to walk on it to sniff, the grouch would yell at you like you'd closed his tail in the sliding door.

I checked out Nelly's yard once more. Something didn't look right, but I couldn't put my paw on the problem. Roxie said she heard something scraping or dragging, then the glass broke, then later on she heard the howl from Nelly. I lifted my rear leg and scratched my ribs and thought about that. It's hard to think ahead or even remember much stuff.

Victor's side yard had a bunch of planting garbage piled in one corner. I saw some old plant buckets, a wheelbarrow, and some rakes and shovels. None of this landscape stuff was unusual, he was always raking leaves or fixing-up something in the yard. Me and Meatloaf know all about that. Sometimes we watch Robert replace shrubs that die after we dig up their water lines.

I trotted down the hall to the front bedroom to see what was happening out there. The view was great. I could see everything in the subdivision, even cars and trucks on the big street that went by our neighborhood. Cars were driving in and out, trucks were bringing packages and worker-humans. The garbage truck was pickin' up over on the next block, and the neighbor across the street was having his trees trimmed. And down at the park, the city workers were shortening the grass. Mostly, one was working and four were watching him work.

I got down from the window and nosed around the bedroom. This was the room that friends stayed in when they came to visit. It still smelled like—

Woof! Woof! Woof!

Catcrap.

Humans were home.

I raced down the hall, flew down the stairs and planted my butt on the floor next to Meatloaf. I heard the big garage door moving, then the trunk of a car closed. I knew Robert drove one of those Jeep cars with no trunk, so this had to be our female coming home. I wasn't thrilled about it. She was OK, but not as cool as Robert.

Her name is Judy. Actually she calls herself Judith, but I'm from the Westside and I can't say that name. She moved here from some big city far away, and I don't think she's adjusted to desert living yet. When we bring a dried lizard or dead pigeon into the house, she screams and dances all around. Not cool at all.

I like her music, though. She plays this nice, soothing music, it even puts me to sleep. Robert's music wakes up everyone, even Meatloaf. Other than that, Judy is a pain to me and Meat. So we treat her like we do the cats in the neighborhood. We keep our distance.

She walked in the house carrying a bag over her shoulder and pulling one of those suitcases with little wheels and a handle. We stuck our noses on the suitcase right away. The smells were great, kinda exotic. I was hoping there was some new kind of dog treat in there for us to sample, but no luck. I guess we could have sampled the suitcase, 'cause it had those nice leather corners, but she always takes it upstairs.

Judy got a glass of water, finished lookin' at the letters and finally spoke to us.

Were you good dogs while I was gone?

They always ask you that, like they think we're gonna confess to chewing a hole in the leather couch or something. First off, they really don't want to know. Trust me. Maybe she was just making conversation. But the minute she noticed we were there and spoke to us, we went over to her and sat right at her feet.

That's when I screwed-up royal.

I don't know why I did this, but she was standing there reading a letter or something and I got this hit, this strange but faint scent off her. It was not her normal aroma. Anyway I wasn't thinking, I wanted to check it out. So I stuck my nose right in her crotch.

She kinda floated up in the air, higher than a dog-food bag. On her way down she whacked me on the snout.

NO! Bad Dog!

She yelled some more, I'm not sure what, but nothin' good. Then she grabbed us both and locked us out in the garage. She wasn't happy at all, but neither was Meatloaf. It was hot in the garage.

"Why'd you do that, dawg? You know they hate that."

"Sorry, Meat. I lost my head for a moment. Didn't you smell that strange odor?"

"The chicken salad?"

"Not her lunch. That other thing."

I should have realized Meatloaf wouldn't have picked it up, his nose isn't as good as mine. Not that he's got a bad nose, it's as good as any other dog. We can smell a dead body underwater. I tried to describe the scent to Meatloaf.

"It's hard to explain. It was a kind of rank, definitely not her normal odor."

"Yeah, well, sometimes she smells funky."

"No, this was different. It wasn't any smell she'd ever had. Did you watch any of that Animal Channel show last week called, Dogs in Medicine?"

"No, but I knew a dog who lived in Mendocino. It's not that far from Fresno. I was born in Fresno."

"This show was about cancer-finding dogs."

"Cancer. Never heard of it. That in California?"

"Cancer's somethin' bad that humans get, somethin' that feeds on them."

"Like tics?"

"Yeah, like tics, but smaller. A lot smaller, and they're called cells. And there's a lot of them eating until the human gets real sick or dies."

"I had tic fever once."

"They're finding out that dogs can smell cancer in human patients. They can smell cancer in a female's breast. In some laboratory tests, dogs can pick out chemical smells in just a few parts per million!"

"They pay these dogs for smelling?"

28

"So I'm a little worried here. I smell her but I also smell something funny in there too. I'm thinkin' maybe she's got some cancer in there, or somethin' else bad is goin' on."

"I don't know, but just don't poke her there anymore."

I heard the shower running upstairs. It looked like we were going to be in there a while, so we lay down next to the door to the house. We tried to sleep, but it was hot and we had to pant now and then.

After a while later Meatloaf sat up. "You think Robert will let us out? I need to pee."

"Listen."

Somebody rang our door bell. We heard female voices, then a person came in our house. I think it was the female who lives across the street, she likes to talk a lot, too. They were talking about the murder at Nelly's. They were plenty excited, talking loud and long. Nothing like a dead body in the neighborhood to shake things up.

FIVE

Robert did let us in, as soon as he got home. That's when we normally get second-meal, after he gets home and changes out of his work clothes. After eating, we left Robert and Judy alone, it seemed like they wanted to talk. We hung out in the yard under the trees, then Meatloaf ate a bunch of seed pods for dessert.

The weather looked like we'd moved into the cooler part of the hot time. That's when we get these tall puffy clouds shootin' way up in the sky, then a warm wind comes in smelling like dirt and rain. This goes on every day or so, sometimes a lot of dirt blows around but no rain comes down. Then later we get a day where it really does rain hard. Sometimes trees blow over in the neighborhood, and little rivers come up in the desert. And the next day we can dig in a lot of places in the yard that were too hard before. Everything smells better, too.

Tonight it just felt breezy and cooler, but I didn't think we'd get any rain.

We considered going in and getting our leash and collar out of the drawer to remind them, but we thought we'd better wait on Robert. Most times, we don't wear a collar. That's because one time Meatloaf got his collar caught in the dog door opening and couldn't get out. Luckily Robert was home and heard him yelpin' and squealin' like a dog losing a cat fight. So now we just put on our collar and leash when we walk or go somewhere special, like to the Vet-human for cold tubes up our butt.

That's fine by me, I hate collars, I don't like wearing one. I know it means our name and address isn't on us most times, 'cause our tag is on the collar, but it's not like we're going to run away from this cushy setup. This is the best home we've ever had.

Finally it started to get darker, so Robert and Judy came to get us for our walk. We got our collars on, then Robert took hold of both our leashes because Judy says we're too much for her or something. When we walked by Nelly's house, I could tell Judy was upset 'cause she just walked on by quick without looking. I noticed the yellow tape over the door was gone but all the lights were out.

We were some of the first dogs to arrive, so me and Meatloaf put our noses to the grass and checked to see who'd been there since last night. All over the park, rabbits ran out from under bushes and disappeared. I didn't even bother chasing them, because it wouldn't look cool to try and have one get away from you. There was a fat concrete pipe through the block fence that let water run into the low grass part of the park. It filled up when it rained hard. That's where the rabbits usually disappear to, in that pipe. Good riddance, I say.

But we needed exercise, so we did a fast lap around the park. Roxie the Fox-Terrier and Gizmo the Jack Russell chased us and blew right by like scalded dogs. Of course, we were holdin' back a little, but there was no way could we catch them, even if we were younger. Then I saw a flash of yellow as Simba ran up to me. We took off runnin' together, neck in neck. I bumped her a little and she bumped me a little, then we stopped to pant and I got a good whiff of her dog breath. I noticed her human bought her the expensive canned dog food. Me and Meatloaf only got that on our birthdays.

Most of the pack was there. I saw Winston the Bulldog jumpin' up and down, so we all went over to him and got in a huddle to talk stuff over.

"Hey," Winston said, panting. "I'm on to something."

"What's up?"

"I ran into that Doberman Pinscher this morning."

I knew Winston's humans were older and didn't go to work anymore, so he went for walks around the neighborhood early in the day.

Gizmo knew about the Doberman. "You mean Spike. From the next street over."

"Uha-uha-uha-uha, Yeah."

Winston was still panting hard, he must have run over here to tell us. I felt sorry for him, I knew Bulldogs didn't handle our heat too well. Meatloaf thought their panting didn't work as good as ours, 'cause they had their nose shoved so far back. Winston's face was kinda weird, I thought maybe his ancestor's eyesight was bad and they ran into too many trees. He said his ancestors were bull baiters, whatever that is.

He continued talking, mixing his panting with his discovery.

"Anyway, uha-uha-uha, we walked by his house today. I asked him where he was from, and he says, uha-uha, Cottonwood, you know, Arizona. Says he's lived there all his life, until a little while ago."

Roxie looked amused. "So what? They got dogs in Cottonwood."

"Not like this one. You ever hear him bark? Spike's got this heavy Brooklyn accent. Bauw Wauw, Bauw Wauw."

"I don't get it," Meatloaf said.

"A Doberman Pinscher named Spike? From Cottonwood? Bauw Wauw? I'm telling you this mutt is witness protection. I bet the U.S. Marshals stashed him and his owner in our quiet little neighborhood. It's the perfect spot."

I hated to poo-poo any of our pack's ideas, but this sounded like Winston's over-active imagination. The dog was always coming up with wild ideas. I kept my real feelings to myself, though. I didn't want to discourage anyone from protecting the neighborhood, so I played along.

"Thanks. That's somethin' we oughta look into, Winston."

He went on. "You never see 'em here with the rest of us at the park, they don't leave their house. I bet they got a shady history. I think his human was a button man."

"Say what?"

"A cleaner. Torpedo. Hatchet man. You, know, a hit man. Probably worked for the mob back there, could have free-lanced."

"Is your human letting you watch the Court TV Channel again, Winston?" Gizmo asked.

There was no stopping him.

"Get this. Spike's human doesn't have a job. When we walk by his house, he's slagging around out in the yard or working on his car or just sittin' on his arse. He's got no mates. There's no skirt living with him."

That didn't seem unusual to Roxie. "Not everyone needs a female, maybe he just likes living alone."

Simba disagreed. "All males need a female. They can't find anything without one."

"Let's say Winston is right," I said, playing along. "You think he's gonna whack somebody in his own neighborhood? He'd be trying to be invisible. Why would he kill Nelly's human?"

"Maybe Nelly peed on his grass," someone said.

We turned toward the new voice. It was Bandit, I hadn't smelled him walk up. And it looked like he'd brought some moral support tonight, 'cause he brought that wimpy poodle, Remi. Remi lived right across the street from Bandit. They made a strange pair.

"Thanks Bandit, but I think we got this handled."

He ignored me. "This is a public park, right Remi?"

Remi was tall for a Miniature Poodle, but he was still the Miniature version. His fur was trimmed in a thin cut, making him look just like what he was—small and thin. I've rarely met a mutt I disliked more, but I tried to stay polite, even when he talked down to us.

"Precisely," Remi stated. "And I have to say I'm concerned about this vigilante mindset your group is promoting in our public park. I think a little restraint is in order, not some kind of animal brute force."

Meatloaf didn't concern himself with manners. He looked at me and asked, "You want me to bite him?"

"This isn't about vigilante justice," I said. "We're just tryin' to work together to keep the neighborhood safe."

Remi sniffed like we were dumber than an inbred Afghan hound. "In my experience, if you leave ruffians alone, they will leave you alone."

Roxie raised a paw. "Wait. We talking about coyotes or killers?"

"What's the difference?" Bandit said.

"There's a big difference," I said. The coyotes are just trying to survive. Nelly's human was murdered by someone evil that could kill any of our humans. Or us."

Remi rolled his weeping eyes. "Evil? Oh, please."

Now I wanted to bite him.

"Let's talk about the bloody hit man," Winston said.

"Winston, cool it, we'll check him out, don't worry." I turned to the doubting duo. "Why don't you two just back off and let us deal with this?"

Bandit and Remi took a few steps outside our group and conversed in low tones. They glanced back with a look of disgust.

I returned to our own conversation. "I got an idea. Why don't we get in Nelly's backyard. If we could get in there and smell around, it would help us figure out what we're up against."

"That sounds like fun," Gizmo said.

"Forget it," Meatloaf said. "Our fences are too tall. It'd be easier to open a can of dog food with your teeth. I know, I've tried it."

Gizmo stuck his chest out. "I can get over her fence. I can get over it and open the gate."

I knew a Jack Russell could jump and climb, but open gates? "How you gonna do that?"

"Gettin' over's no problem. It takes a trick to open the gate, but I can show you."

It seemed like a great idea. "Can you get out in the morning? Out of your yard?"

"Sure," Gizmo said.

"How about real early, just when it starts to get light, you come by our house. Then you and me will go check it out."

"You're on."

Meatloaf didn't look happy about our plan. "Hey wait a minute, dawg. Every time you do this kinda stuff we both get locked up in the garage and I have to hold it forever. My kidneys aren't what they use to be."

"You're right, Meatloaf. It would be easier with less dogs, anyway. You stay home, you can cover for me."

Roxie jumped in. "You want me to come to?"

"No, you live right next door, so you be the lookout. But tell us something, is Nelly's male-human there? Or anyone else?"

"Victor's back, but he's not staying at the house. He came home from his trip the day after the murder with a briefcase and two suitcases. He went in the house a while, then these uniform-humans came in this big truck and went inside with big buckets and all these bottles and cans. It looked like when the cleaning-humans come, but much more serious."

I nodded. Robert didn't have cleaning-humans, but a lot of the neighbors did. "Where'd Victor go?"

"I don't know, but he wasn't staying there last night."

"I wouldn't want to live there anymore if I were him," said Simba. "But please, can we do something about the coyotes? They scare me just as bad. My neighbor's cat disappeared and the humans think coyotes took him."

"My neighbor's cat went tits-up, too," said Winston.

Me and Meatloaf looked at each other. "Simba," I said. "There's nothing to worry about. The coyotes won't bother us."

Gizmo disagreed. "They might not bother you, you're big enough. But they like small dogs as well as they do cats."

"They'll eat big dogs," said Roxie. "Where I used to live, the coyote pack would send one of their females in heat close to the subdivision. Then she'd lure the male dog that came to get her, lure him out far enough away so the pack could jump him. They took a German Shepherd friend I had."

35

"These coyotes wouldn't do that," I said. "We're like brothers."

"Actually, I think we're more like distant cousins," said Remi.

The doubting duo was back.

Bandit sneered at me. "You're out in the neighborhood playing police dog while we've got a bigger problem right out there in the desert. We should be guarding our houses against these vicious coyotes."

Simba and some others in the pack nodded muzzles.

I raised my voice. "No!"

Bandit looked down his snout. "I don't think you know what you're barking about, Basset ears."

I really wanted to bite that dog.

"Coyotes are not the real threat, bone-breath."

He turned and looked toward the mountain. "We'll see."

Just then we heard a commotion in the group of our humans. Some of them were raising their voices and waving their arms. This wasn't normal, it looked like they were all upset about the murder, too.

"Hey, Meatloaf. Taser. Looks like your humans are fighting."

Winston was right. It was Judy and Robert who were making the ruckus. I watched them argue, then suddenly Judy walked away alone, back toward our house.

"Well, isn't that nice," a female dog commented.

That puff ball Bichon Fries, Buffy, had joined us. She stood between Bandit and Remi, then commented again about my human's argument.

"So now we have vulgar public displays of temper. One has to wonder about the breeding of some of these humans," she said.

I was tired of all this negative feedback. I nodded at Meatloaf and Gizmo, turned away from the group and trotted back to Robert. At times like this, I wished I was back on the Westside.

***

They'd been arguing for a while. It wasn't the first time they'd argued, but this was probably the longest. Judy seemed to be doing

36

most of the yelling, but usually she does most of the talking, so I guess that was normal for her kind.

I don't understand this human mating business.

I'm not sure how long Judy and Robert have been together, but I haven't seen any pups around here, so I don't know why they mated to begin with. They're such different humans. Robert is like me, an Arizona guy, born right here in the desert. Judy was born far away and lived in a big city where everybody says a lot of words. I think she moved out here to work and say words. When she talks, most of the time it's about work-this and work-that, or else it's about this human or that human.

Robert usually holds the papers in front of his face when she talks, then every once in a while he puts the papers down and says, really, or something like that.

They seem like male and female types, but from different breeds. Robert is a down to earth English Setter, but Judy is more of a skittish Italian Greyhound. I think they better be careful if they ever do have any pups, they could be in for a real surprise. At least, that's my experience with dog mating. Mount anything that moves and you might end up with a pup lookin' like a Welsh Corgi. That poor thing's got legs shorter than a Rottweiler's leash in a crowd of old ladies.

Meatloaf seems more open about mating, as he is about most things. He's from the country of California, wherever that is. He's a bit of a layback, but still a good guy. He likes to lie around in the day-light and chill a lot, and he's real big on eating.

We were layin' low outside the house, waiting for the yellin' to stop, so none of it came our way. This is basic dog survival stuff. I tried not to listen, because I hate when humans get mad and argue. I'm a Labrador, I need to be happy.

Meatloaf don't seem to care one way or another. He got up and started eatin' seed pods from the trees. I watched him for a while, trying to figure out why he liked them. They tasted like wood to me.

"Why do you eat those, things, buddy?"

"They fill me up. And I get a little hit off 'em."

"A hit?"

"Yeah. Mellows me out. Kinda like the mushrooms that used to grow in my backyard in Fresno."

It was hard to imagine Meatloaf needing more mellow. Maybe that's important for California dogs. But this country was different.

"How long you been in Arizona, Meatloaf?"

"I dunno. Human before last."

"You know, this is Scottsdale. Our humans might drink a little alcohol now and then, but we're big on fitness. Trim bodies. Healthy food."

"I'm into all that."

I point to the seed pods on the ground. "What about all these pods?"

"Seed pods are healthy."

"How you figure?"

"They make me poop regular."

"They make you fat."

He looked insulted. "So? That's an added benefit. A dog needs a little fat in reserve, because you never know if these dumb humans are gonna forget to feed you."

The voices inside the house got louder. Finally I couldn't stand it anymore, I went over and put my ear close to the dog door. I sat and listened until I understood the argument. Finally Meatloaf saw me sitting there and got curious.

"That Judy yelling? What's she saying?" he asked.

"Uhhhhhh."

"Taser."

I tried to form the words but nothing came out.

"Taser. What's she saying?"

Please, not that.

SIX

I see Mike throw the tennis ball and I take off. It's up in the air a long time, shootin' in a big arc to the far end of the school yard. It bounces once, twice, and then I grab it while it's still in the air. I jog back, takin' my time, tryin' to pant with the ball stuffed in my mouth, getting it all slimy.

I don't give it to him right away, I try to catch my breath before I have to run again. Finally I drop it at his feet and do some more panting. It's not very hot out, just a little bit. Mostly it's wet. The grass is soaked from the rain a little time ago, my human's shoes are soaked, too.

I'm ready now. I stare at him, waiting, ready to run. But he's just lookin' around, the ball is still at his feet. He doesn't seem to want to play anymore.

Let's go, Chili.

So we start to walk back to the car and I look, and I see he's left the ball sitting in the wet grass. I figure maybe it's not good anymore, maybe it's too slimy. I jump in the back seat and sit on the towel Mike put down. Mike's careful with his cars. We had a nicer one before, but even though this one smells old, it works plenty good. If he fixed the dents and got some new paint it would be even better.

We come to this grass schoolyard when I need exercise, it's the biggest field we've got in this neighborhood. Our yard has grass, but it's not big enough to play and run around very much. The bad thing is, sometimes pup-humans are on the school grass, so we have to wait for those days when they're not here.

I look out the car window as we drive along. I love this neighborhood, all the humans are so friendly and nice. But some of my best dog buddies have moved away, and nobody has moved back in their houses yet. When they do, I hope they have a dog.

We pull in the driveway and open the garage door. It's pretty empty in the garage right now. Mike and Sandy have been having garage sales a lot, and they sold a lot of stuff, even most of the furniture in our house. But that's no problem for me, I sleep on the floor anyway.

I go in the front with Mike and we head to the kitchen for a drink of water, and I see Sandy has a pizza box and two cans of something. They sit at the counter on stools, 'cause they sold the kitchen table at one of those garage sales. Mike puts a small slice of pizza on the floor for me. I look at Sandy first, 'cause she hates when Mike does that, but she doesn't say anything this time. So I eat it quick before she changes her mind.

When I look at her again I see she's doin' that human thing with the sad face and the wet eyes. Mike puts his arm around her, but they don't say 'nothin. She's been doin' that a lot lately, but at least they don't argue. I hate when my humans argue.

Mike and Sandy never do.

After dinner we go out front. They walk over to the neighbor across the street, but Mike tells me to stay. I hate that word, stay. You miss out on all the fun, and I'm a Labrador, I need all I can get.

They stand and talk at the neighbor's door awhile, then they shake hands and hug, and then they go to the neighbor next door to us and do the same thing. I get bored and start lookin' for little lizards under bushes. I can usually spot them and chase them, but I've never caught one yet, they're too fast. I find 'em dead sometimes, but then they're all hard and brittle so I leave them alone. It's no fun unless they run away.

Pretty soon we go back in the house. Mike and Sandy sit in these cool plastic lawn chairs and watch this little television that's sittin' on the floor. These chair legs are great to chew on, kinda soft but kinda hard. There's teeth marks on almost every leg, I'm proud to say. I go to sleep next to them because I'm dog-tired from all the running at the school yard.

I hear them get up later and go to their room to sleep, so I go sleep on the living room rug, my favorite place. You can hear everything that happens, inside and out. Later I heard Mike get up. It's dark out everywhere but not close to first meal, so I don't know what's up. Mike's just walking around the house, not doin' anything. He walks around and stops, then walks around and stops. Finally he comes over and lays down right next to me on the floor.

He doesn't want to play, he just stays there with me. I stick my paw on his arm and we lay there the rest of the dark-time.

When it gets light outside we all get up. Mike goes in their room and after a while comes out with some suitcases and small boxes. Mike puts them in the trunk of the car and then he and Sandy look all around the house. They give me some water and a piece of pizza from last night, which seems like a very special treat for first-meal.

Then we all head for the car. I jump in the backseat on the towel. I'm not expecting a trip today so I'm kind of excited, but after a while I get tired of watching all the cars and buildings and I put my head down. I sleep a little while they drive.

Some time later we stop at this big building in Phoenix somewhere. I can smell all kinds of dogs, a lot of different dogs, so many mutts my nose is goin' crazy. We go in the front door and I hear a lot of crazy barking and I smell a lot of crazy smells. Mike talks to the lady at the desk, then after a while we go in this little room together.

Then Mike gets down and hugs me and talks quietly about stuff I don't understand. He says stuff about our house and four closings and no-work and small apartment and no-dogs, but that's all I the words I understand, until he says; We'll be back.

I know those words. They make me feel good.

We'll be back.

Mike and Sandy say them to me when they go out in the dark-time or they go to work or they go to the store and leave me alone.

They say; We'll be back. Then I know they'll come back to me.

So I don't worry much when the strange man comes with a leash and takes me out of the room, 'cause I see Mike standing there and he says those words to me again.

We'll be back.

SEVEN

"Taser. What's she saying?"

I was having a hard time hearing anything. I couldn't hear Judy or Robert any more, just a loud buzz in my head.

"Taser."

Meatloaf's voice seemed far away, like I was floating above him. Finally I looked up.

"Yeah?"

"What's goin' on, Taser?"

"She wants to move."

"So what's the problem? Let her go back to where she came from."

"She wants to move with Robert and all their stuff."

"I don't wanna move again. I like it out here."

"She wants to sell the house and move to the city. Move to an apartment downtown in the city."

Meatloaf thought about what that meant. "The Phoenix city? What'd Robert say?"

"He doesn't want to move. That's why they're yelling."

"I don't like the city."

"She says she can't live in a neighborhood with a murder right down the street."

"I don't think she ever liked it here."

"She says she doesn't feel safe here any more."

Meatloaf thought. "You know, I never really liked her."

"They won't take us, Meat."

"You know something else, I don't think she likes me, either."

"They're gonna take us to the pound and leave us and not come back."

Meatloaf looked over with a jerk. "What?"

"They won't take us with them. If they move to a city apartment, they won't take us. Apartments are no-dogs."

"You're talkin' strange, buddy."

I was feelin' strange. I went out to the backyard to sit and figure out what I did bad. My stomach hurt, so I ate some grass.

Meatloaf came out and sat with me. He ate a little grass in sympathy.

"Let's not worry about this, it may not happen. Robert wants to stay here so maybe we won't move."

"You don't get it. We're in trouble."

"You got too much negative energy, dawg. We'll think of something. Use that brain, you got a good brain."

"It's no use." Suddenly, it came to me. "Yeah. We can fix this, Meatloaf."

"Grass can't fix everything."

"It's the murder."

"What about it?"

"We have to find out who did this and catch him. We have to find out who murdered her human and get the police to take him away. Then she'll feel safe."

"Forget the grass, Taser. Eat some seed pods and mellow out."

"No, listen. I'm going with Gizmo in the morning to look at Nelly's house. Maybe we'll find something."

Meatloaf cocked his head to the side. "Find somethin' the police didn't?"

"Meat. Come on. They're only human."

***

When Robert went to bed we both got our dog bone treats, then he went upstairs to bed. Judy was already up there messin' around. Just like I'd been doing for days, I took my bone outside and stuck it through the fence for the nursing coyote. When I turned around,

Meatloaf was standing right there in the yard with his bone still in his mouth, untouched. He stuck his through the fence where I'd put mine.

Meatloaf didn't say anything, he just turned around and went inside to sleep. I followed him through the dog door and lay on the rug, too, but I couldn't doze until much later. It wasn't a good sleep. My legs kicked and jerked to wicked nightmares that seemed all too real.

ZEUS!

KILL!

My head jerked up off the floor, I was panting fast and furious. I lay my head down and tried to slow my breathing. I closed my eyes, then finally fell into a deep sleep.

When something woke me up much later, I didn't even know which human's house I was in, I was so tired. I lifted my head to look at the window, the light outside was very faint. Then I remembered.

Gizmo!

I glanced over at Meatloaf. "Cover for me." He mumbled something but didn't move.

I ran out the dog door and along the house to the front gate. Gizmo was dancing impatiently, waiting for me to come out.

"Let's go, Taser!"

"How do I get out?"

"Look up. On the gate, see that shiny gray metal thing?"

"Got it."

"It's the latch. You just jump up and flip it with your nose."

"I can't jump that high."

"Sure you can, try it. You got to flip and push on the gate at the same time."

I hunched down and jumped. Nope. It seemed like I wasn't getting any higher then Gizmo. I tried again. Nope. The latch seemed farther away than those New York bagels sittin' on top of our refrigerator.

The athletic little Jack Russell wasn't impressed with my jumping, and said so.

"You suck, dude."

"Hey, I'm a swimmer, not a jumper. You wouldn't be so critical if you were drowning."

"Try this," he said. "Pretend you're jumping on a human. Pretend you're jumping up and knocking them down."

Oh yeah. Judy's mother at Thanksgiving. But that's another, No-No, Bad Dog, story.

I tried it and got close. "Almost."

"Get a run at."

I backed up two dog-lengths, ran, leaped and scratched myself up the gate and flipped the latch. The wood gate sprung open and almost whacked Gizmo in the head. I landed in the front yard. We left it open a little so I could get back in.

"Let's go," said Gizmo.

We started creepin' to Nelly's, stayin' close to the house and away from the street so we wouldn't be too obvious. As if dogs creeping through neighborhood yards wasn't obvious.

"Wait." I stopped in front of our house.

"What's wrong?" asked Gizmo.

"I don't have my collar on. I don't have my name tag."

"Don't worry about it, we're not going to Tucson, we're just going to Nelly's place."

I kept goin' but I didn't like it 'cause I felt naked. We almost got past Harley the Rottweiler's house without waking him up, but just then a car turned and came down our street. We lay flat on his gravel lawn and didn't flinch. It wasn't very light out, so the car had its headlights on as it drove slowly down our street. An arm stuck out the driver's window holding somethin' white.

Thud.

Thud.

"It's the papers-human," I told Gizmo. "Pretend you're a rabbit."

Thud.

Thud.

The car went around the corner and disappeared. We kept creepin'. Next was Roxie's house but we knew she wouldn't bark. When we went by her fence gate, she was standing there waggin' her tail. She lifted one paw and gave us the toes-up sign.

Since they shared the same side-yard fence, Nelly's gate was just a few dog-lengths from Roxie's gate. I checked for the latch, then realized it was on the inside. It looked like we were stopped in our tracks.

"Now what?" I asked Gizmo.

"Not a problem, water dog."

It was the craziest thing I'd ever seen dog do—except the time Meatloaf ate ten-pounds from the open dog-food bag. Gizmo ran right at the house, jumped and hit the wall, then bounced up to the top of the block fence. He balanced there, then he hopped down into the side yard.

"Stand back," he said.

He jumped way up and nosed at the latch. It took him three tries but it opened right up. I joined Gizmo inside their yard.

"What're we looking for?" he asked.

"I don't know, just look. But stay away from the other side of the house, Bandit lives over there."

We went right to the backyard, past the planting stuff I'd already seen from the upstairs window at my house. We trotted over to the swimming pool and stood on the deck. The water looked gray, nothing like our drinking water at home. It didn't smell as clean, either. Behind us was a tile patio connected to the house, just like in our backyard. Except here the patio and the patio furniture here were covered with dirt from the wind storms.

"Over here."

Gizmo was standing at the very rear, looking out the view fence. "Look, I can see your backyard fence."

I went back and saw it too, the houses were all against the desert, you could see inside our yard a little. I smelled the metal fence; it had the odor of ten different humans so it didn't tell me anything.

"Gizmo, you get anything off the fence?"

He put his nose to it. "Humans, none distinctive. Nobody I think is important."

I turned around and looked at Nelly's house. One of the rear windows had a big piece of wood over it.

"That must be what Roxie heard, breaking glass from this window. I'll bet the killer came over this fence from somewhere out in the desert."

Gizmo nodded.

I was getting' nervous, it was getting light and we didn't have much time. I glanced around, hoping to find something that looked wrong. I couldn't see anything. So I thought maybe the normal stuff would point us in the right direction. I sniffed the trees in the backyard and picked up a disgusting scent. It turned my stomach.

"Gizmo, you smell anything funny around here? Is that human blood?"

He trotted over to a big plastic bag by the wheelbarrow, it was half-empty. "I don't know about blood, but his bag smells rotten." He stuck his snout in the bag and moved the plastic. "It's ground-up poop."

The smell upset me so much, I thought I might throw up. "Hey cover that up, will you? It's gonna make me puke."

"Taser, you're such a lightweight."

"Must be my sensitive nose. I ever tell you I've got Bluetick Hound blood in me?"

"And that's why your ears are big and so on and so on. Only about ten times."

"So what is that stuff?"

"It's poop from cows, called manure. It makes your grass healthy and grey. I went with my human to the home store once and got some for our lawn. Believe me, it stinks worse when it's wet."

There was nothin' left out here to investigate. Nothin' but the dog door on the patio. I made my decision.

"Hey Gizmo."

"We gonna leave now?"

"We gotta go in."

"In the house? No way, Taser. I didn't sign on for that."

"Come on, we gotta see inside."

He backed up. "You maybe, not me."

"Gizmo, something's changed. My humans are talkin' about selling the house and getting away from this neighborhood. Judy's freaked out."

"That stinks."

"This ain't for fun anymore. I gotta find out who did this and try to catch the guy. Then maybe they won't move."

"I don't know. I think it's too risky inside, you can get trapped real easy. I mean, if a human can die, we can die."

"OK Gizmo, I'll go in, you watch out."

I trotted up and stuck my nose through the dog door.

"Watch out for what?" Gizmo asked.

I didn't answer, I was already halfway inside. It was a tight squeeze, Nelly was a beagle—smaller than me—so her door was smaller too. I got in and stood in their kitchen. The first hit I got was chemical cleaners, then the blood invaded my nose. I stopped and retched on the floor but nothing came up. I stood there for a moment, feeling dizzy.

I hate blood.

I walked through the kitchen, then I took a quick look around the living room. They only had a downstairs house, there was no stairs going to rooms above. Some houses in the neighborhood had an upstairs, some didn't.

I didn't have much time, I had to move quickly and separate the scents. I sniffed high and low. I could smell a lot of humans, some from my neighborhood, some strangers. There'd been a lot of males in here recently and it was confusing me.

I went down the hall to the bedrooms next. I padded quietly, wondering what bedroom the murder must have happened in. I peeked around the corner of the first door-opening. Nope. It had a desk, a chair, a computer and a bookcase. There was no bed and no blood smell, but something smelled funny, not right. I made a pass through but couldn't locate it, there were so many new smells.

I continued down the hall. The second door-opening was a bedroom, but it looked like the visitor bedroom we had at our house. All I saw was a flowered bedspread on a big bed. I could smell different humans in there, even my own humans.

Then I picked up something that smelled like chemicals, but different from the cleaners. I sniffed around the bed and finally ended up at the trash can. No, it wasn't in the trash can, but beside it on the floor. I moved the can with my nose, almost underneath was a small white strip of plastic. I sniffed it carefully. Somewhere in my brain it registered as important. I tried to pick it up with my teeth, but it was flat on the floor. I licked it and it stuck to my tongue. I ran to the kitchen dog door with it, stuck it through and dropped it on the patio.

"Whazzat?" Gizmo asked.

"We're taking it with us, but I'm not done looking yet."

"Hurry up," Gizmo said.

I went back down the hallway. There was only one room left.

It was the big bedroom at the end of the hall. It creeped me out just thinkin' about the horrible thing that happened in there, but I had to go in and look.

I walked to the open doorway. I saw their bed. There were no covers or sheets or anything on it. In this room the smell of her blood was the strongest. I sat down, repulsed by the odor. I didn't think I could do it.

But I had to try.

I walked closer, then stopped. The smells were overpowering. I retched again. I tried to put the blood and chemicals out of my nose and just smell the rest. I looked down. The floor seemed like it had different colored areas, blotchy grey, light grey, dark grey—my eyes were useless here. I had to use my nose, my nose was better than everything.

What would the police have missed?

I sniffed the dresser. I sniffed the table. I went in the bathroom and sniffed. Nothin'. Nothin'. Nothin'.

"Taser!"

It was Gizmo. Somethin' must be up, we probably needed to get goin'.

But I went back to the bedroom dresser and sniffed each drawer, thinking they might have missed something. I could tell her female scent, then his male scent. I smelled all the different stinky stuff the females put on their bodies.

"Taser!"

Maybe someone was coming. I trotted down the hall, then skidded to a stop at the room with the desk and the chair. Sniff, sniff. I went inside to look one more time, something was definitely there. Sniff. It was the desk. Sniff, sniff. I thought the chemical smell might have messed up my nose. Something in a closed bottom drawer smelled strange but familiar. I grabbed the knob with my teeth and pulled it all the way out, then looked inside.

The drawer had a soft leather briefcase in it. I sniffed it close, but it only made me more confused.

"Taser! Now!"

I had to know if I was right, but I was out of time. I had to take it with me.

I bit the briefcase handle and dragged it out of the drawer. It wasn't heavy but it was awkward. I struggled with it down the hall and into the kitchen. Gizmo had his head stuck through the dog door, talkin' fast.

"Let's go! Bandit's awake next door."

I tried to get the briefcase through the dog-door opening but it was tight. I pushed and jiggled it around. It was gettin' heavier or I was gettin' tired.

Bow Wow! Bow Wow! Bow Wow! Bow Wow!

Bandit. He was rattin' us out to the whole neighborhood. That dog is such a weasel.

Bow Wow! Bow Wow!

Gizmo was frantic. "We gotta go! What are you doin' with that?"

"I need it." I pushed on the briefcase, but it seemed too tight a fit.

Bow Wow! Bow Wow!

"Pull, Gizmo."

Gizmo sunk his teeth in it and pulled from the outside. It moved, then caught on its handle.

Bow Wow! Bow Wow!

"It's stuck, just leave it!" Gizmo said.

"I can't get outta here now, we gotta get it past the door."

He pulled and I pushed, finally it went through. I quickly followed.

'Where's the plastic thing, Gizmo?"

"We should go, right now."

"No, get it!"

Gizmo bent down and got the plastic strip in his mouth.

Bow Wow! Bow Wow! Bow Wow!

I bolted for the gate, holdin' the briefcase high. Gizmo was right behind me. I stopped out front and waited while Gizmo put his front paws on Nelly's gate and pushed it shut.

Then we ran for it.

Bow Wow! Bow Wow! Bow Wow!

Bandit wouldn't shut his snout.

Then Harley started barking.

Woof! Woof! Woof! Woof!

Catcrap.

We ran as fast as we could with our booty. We ran across all the front yards to my gate opening. Gizmo stopped long enough to spit out the plastic strip, then he closed the gate and ran towards his home. I sat there panting, listening to dogs bark all up and down the street. If the neighborhood humans weren't up yet, this would wake a few. I hoped Gizmo got home all right.

Meatloaf burst out the dog door to meet me, then stopped short at the sight of the soft leather briefcase. "What the heck is that?"

When I caught my breath, I told him.

"I think it's a big clue, I'm not sure what. I'm not sure I want to know. But we gotta hide it before Robert or Judy gets up. Help me get it in the dog house."

EIGHT

Robert loaded our water dishes and three plastic bottles of water in the Jeep in preparation for our hike. It was still early, not hot yet, but we knew what was coming. We'd had first meal and fresh water and done our business so we were ready to go, past ready, actually. We hopped in the backseat as excited as Labs at a third-grader's birthday party. We knew it would be a good rubber-shoe day when Robert appeared at the top of the stairs, but we didn't know we'd get to go hiking with him. The first clue was when he put our collars on.

He backed the Jeep out of the garage and drove down our quiet street. Most of the houses and yards in our subdivision looked like ours, some had a section of fresh gray grass, but most had desert plants and granite rock with a couple trees here or there. Robert calls our yards 'Disney Desert', whatever that is.

I've seen the new subdivisions go up around here. They come with big machines and dig up all the desert trees and scrape off all the plants until the ground is flat. Then they build houses like ours with those tile roofs. Then the humans go to the home store and buy new desert trees and new desert plants and new rocks until it looks kinda like the desert they just scraped off, except flatter.

So I figured that's why we're hikin' today, to see some real desert before the Disney-humans get there.

Robert had a hat and short pants on and these dark glass-things over his eyes. I could smell the coconut skin-lotion that tastes so good to lick off his skin.

This musta been a rubber-shoe day for a lot of humans, because I saw a lot of them in the neighborhood walking dogs or pushing those wheel carts with pups in them. When we got to the end of our street, I could see Simba stretched out on her grass while her master washed his new black pickup truck. This truck had these huge shiny wheels with giant tires on 'em. It made me wanna lift a leg just lookin' at them.

I stuck my head out the window and barked big-time at Simba. Robert stopped the Jeep to talk with her male, so I seized da carp, like they say. That's Latin, I think, from the History Channel.

I sat up in the back seat, tryin' to look as tough and tasty as a fresh rawhide bone. I used my most macho voice on her.

"Hey good lookin'."

She stretched slow and seductive as she got up. Then she ambled over to the Jeep on those long, long legs. Her well-groomed coat shined bright in the morning day-light.

"Where you boys off to?"

"Hikin'." I jerked my head toward the mountains. "We're takin' Robert up to some tough trails we know in the McDowell's. We want to make sure he gets home all right. You know these humans, they couldn't find their way out of a dog-food bag."

Simba showed her sharp teeth and soft tongue, panting a little as she looked me over. She tossed her head back. "Catch any killers today?"

"Gizmo and I went over the crime scene with a fine-bristle brush, but it looked as clean as Meatloaf's food bowl. We're not done analyzing things yet, so it's best not to talk about it. We should probably keep things—confidential."

"Oh. I understand perfectly, confidential is my middle name." She winked at me.

It was time to leave, Robert revved his motor.

Mine was already revved.

She backed up to the sidewalk. "Have a good day, Meatloaf. And maybe I'll see you at the park later, Mr. Taser."

"Countin' on it."

We drove off toward the subdivision exit.

Meatloaf looked over at me. "I don't know about Simba, dawg. You might want to think twice before you get involved."

"Why? What's wrong with her?"

"There's nothing wrong. She's hot. But that's the problem, yellow-hairs are too high-maintenance. All their life they've been told how cute they are. They think they don't have to try at all, they just fall back on their looks."

"Simba seems perfectly nice."

"Sure, until they sign the breeding papers. Then they turn into psycho bitch. You want to go lighter, what's wrong with a nice Chocolate Lab?"

"I don't know, I'm kinda down on brown. I mean, why do they have to call themselves 'Chocolate'. What's wrong with 'Brown'? It's like they think they're better than Blacks. Do we call ourselves Ebony Labradors?"

"I see your point," said Meatloaf. "How about Roxie?"

"I dunno, I guess she's not my type."

"Mine either. What's her story, anyway?"

"What story? She seems like a nice girl to me."

"No, I mean, do you think she likes males? She seems a little gender-neutral."

"What's that mean?"

"I mean she's in the pack with a bunch of males, yet she never comes on to us. She never acts like she's interested. Is she fixed or what?"

"Maybe we're not her type."

"Sure, but most females would flirt a little, at least sometime. We've known her since we got here and she always seems like just one of the guys."

I thought about it. "Well, I have to admit, I've never considered mounting her."

"I think about mounting every female I meet."

"Me too, it's some kind of biological thing."

"What about a Yellow Lab?"

"They're OK, but a Yellow Lab seems more like a sister. A Golden Retriever is intriguing, exotic, wild. Kinda like Lassie gone bad."

"Now you're talking."

"I bet she's a howler."

"Think so?"

"Bet on it."

"Woof."

***

Robert drove north toward the mountains. I think we were going to his close-by hiking trail, the one a lot of humans in the neighborhood used. It was a wide trail, not steep at first but got steeper as you went. The different thing about this hiking trail was that dogs could come along with humans. I knew we weren't going too far, it was still gonna get hot and we were a little out of shape.

I thought about breakfast time this morning. Our humans didn't seem mad at each other, there was no yelling or mad faces. Maybe Robert had won the house-selling argument.

I nudged Meatloaf with my nose. He was still looking out the window.

"Did you see?"

"What, we missed the turnoff?"

"They didn't argue this morning."

He turned toward me. "What about that burnt-bagel fight?"

"Sure, that, but at least they didn't argue about selling the house."

"Oh."

I waited. "What do you think that means?"

"That bagels are more important."

"No, really."

"He burnt the only cranberry ones we had. That's important."

"Maybe they won't sell after all."

Meatloaf shrugged. "Maybe. Robert likes the desert. I think he'll stay here."

"Maybe she'll move herself," I offered.

"She's got cancer tics, anyway. Let her go."

57

"That's terrible, Meatloaf."

"Too bad, I'm mad at her this morning."

"About wanting to move? Me too."

"About throwing them away. You think I care if they're burnt?"

"I don't know about eating that black stuff, Meatloaf. I heard burnt carbon gives you cancer."

"Forget it, then. I don't want to end up like Judy."

Meatloaf's the same breed as me but a mix of types. Labradors are either English type or American type. The American Lab is tall and lanky, the English Lab is medium height and heavier. They're shorter and wider—like me. Meatloaf's a mix of the two, he's tall and he's heavy. I guess that's why he's always hungry.

We finally reached the little parking area at the bottom of the trail. Other cars and trucks were parked there too. Robert waved to one of our neighbors—Brian, I think his name was.

We jumped out of the Jeep and stood by it while Robert got this belt he puts on with water bottles and a pouch with first-aid stuff in it, stuff for stickers and cuts. It smelled like he had some granola bars in case we might need 'em, which we would for sure if you asked me or Meatloaf.

Neighbor Brian came over to the Jeep. It looked like he was going to hike with us a while, which is fine by me, he's dog-friendly. He bent down, petted us and scratched behind our ears. We got all goofy about it, then Robert took one of the water bottles and wet me and Meatloaf down so we wouldn't get too warm. That's the problem with havin' a black coat in the sun—you get hot real quick. That's even after me sheddin' about a million black hairs on our tile floor the last couple months. Two million if you add in Meatloaf's.

We lined up behind Robert and Brian and started up the trail. The ground was hard; kinda rocky and gravelly, but our pads were pretty tough from running in the street and digging in the yard. So many people had come up here before us that we knew where to step. The rocks were small on the trail, kinda like our neighborhood desert lawns.

The only problem was, Meatloaf limped a little with that shoulder, so I knew we wouldn't get far from the Jeep.

The few desert trees lining the trail were scraggy but still alive. It only took a little rain for them to live, but even that had been scarce lately. I thought about the coyotes and wondered how they survived in such a harsh world.

The thing you gotta watch out for in the desert is cactus, especially those Cholla cactus. You only need to sniff them one time and wham, right in the nose. It hurts worse than a swipe from a cornered cat. Other than that, we just seem to avoid cactus needles naturally, like we got radar or somethin'. I've only been stuck in the leg once.

Needles in your paw pads are a different deal. We get those all the time up here, but Robert brings a little pair of pliers along for the tough cases.

So I'm cruising along, lookin' down at the hill and up the trail a bit, just in case of mountain lions or somethin', and I realize Brian and Robert are talkin' about Nelly's female murder. Usually I ignore humans when they talk. It's mostly stuff you don't want to hear—stuff about their work business or humans you don't know, or commands you don't want to obey. Like 'sit'. So I tune 'em out.

But now I'm listenin' good, 'cause I heard the word murder. Uh huh. Uh huh. Victor upset. Uh huh. Now I'm learnin' some good stuff. No suspect. No clues. No murder weapon. Uh huh. Uh huh. Only camera stolen. I make a memory to tell Gizmo and the pack so we can use this in our investigation.

Then Brian said somethin about Nelly livin' with friends. I hope that meant she was all right.

By then Meatloaf and I were panting like puppies on their first trip to the park. It's cooler up in the McDowell foothills, but when you're black and the day-light's shining, it's never Labrador cool. We're from Newfoundland originally, right there on the North Atlantic Sea. That's why we got two coats of hair. And that's why our hair falls out here like seed pods in the hot-time.

Brian went up the trail alone while we stopped to sit and rest under a drooping Palo Verde tree. Finally we all got a chunk of that granola bar. A little breeze came up and it seemed much nicer. Robert wet us down again and I drank some of the best-tasting water I ever had from his cupped hand.

He put his arm around us both and we looked out on the valley. Heat waves rising made the whole city shake like a wet dog. Dust devils twirled across the dry desert floor below us. A pair of hawks tilted and soared high up in the sky, while my heart soared right there on the ground. I don't know what Robert was thinkin', but I knew I never wanted to be anywhere else but with him and Meatloaf.

Things were goin' so great, I couldn't hardly believe my luck.

That's when I started to worry.

NINE

City of Phoenix Dog Pound

Not too long after first-meal, the clanging starts. The noise is the first thing you notice in the Pound, because it's the worst thing. Steel gates slam on steel cages with nothing to soften the sound but hard concrete and more steel. There's barking that never quits, noise that never sleeps. It's enough to make you as batty. For some of these dogs, it does.

The guard is closer to my cage door now. She's releasing only the dogs on my side of the Pound, one by one. Finally she gets to me and my gate pops open.

Time for exercise.

She's a nice human, but like all the other guards, she acts like she'd rather be somewhere else. I don't get enough love or touching from any of them. They're always too busy doing something else, like smoking a cigarette or talking to each other. I miss Mike and Sandy. I wish they'd come and get me, it seems like they've been gone a long time, but I have no way of knowing for sure.

With my door open and I amble down the hall to the exercise yard. The Pound building is gigantic. The front has all the dog cages, in the back is an exercise and poop place. The whole building stinks like dog business, I wish they'd clean it up better, like Sandy did at our house. I never smelled anything there.

They let half the dogs out at one time, then we go back in and the other half comes out. I guess that's so it doesn't get too crazy in the yard, it's wild enough with half of us runnin' around. I walk slowly out

61

to the big room, I'm not gonna run. I'm in no hurry to get out there with those animals.

My bite places seem to be better, they don't hurt too bad now. They put stitches in that big one on my back where the Vet shaved the hair off. I bet it looks funny.

I see most of the dogs are already out, sniffing the floor, walkin' around. The mutt they call Mad Marmaduke is singing and dancing, some dogs are watching him for entertainment. I feel sorry for Marmaduke, but I don't blame the inmates, there's nothing else to do in here. Mealtimes are the highlight of our day, but since they never give you enough to eat, it seems like you're always hungry.

I take my usual spot against the far wall. I don't run around in the yard, 'cause if you stray into another dog's area they can get mean and angry and make trouble for you. There's a lot of dogs in here, strange-looking types, I don't know what breed they are 'cause they're all mixed together. Some of them are loony, some are just mean.

I met a couple of nice mutts before, but they left soon after they came in, I never got their names. I know a German Shepherd named Major, but everyone knows Major. He's the alpha dog in here, but I'm not sure how much longer he can be on top. He's old, with a lot of white hair on his muzzle, but he can really fight. Sometimes the new dogs challenge him to battle, but he always wins. Experience over age, I guess.

"You're in my spot."

I look up and see a tall mass of bristling hair. It's an Akita I've never seen before. He's still clean, that means he's new here. He looks pure bred. His coat sticks out all over, making him look bigger than he his, but he's still much bigger than me. He's got a bad attitude for a new dog, he seems angry. He probably doesn't want to be here, either.

I ask politely. "Excuse me?"

"You're in my spot. Beat it, big ears."

He towers over me and shows his teeth. He's a head taller and about a hundred scary-lookin' pounds. I'm not messin' with him.

"Sorry."

I move down about ten dog-lengths. It's not as nice a spot, but it looks safe and it's empty. I glance at the mutts wandering around and talkin' to themselves. They don't act like any neighborhood dog I ever met. I try not to make eye contact with them, that's how I got these stitches. Then I hear a voice speak directly to me.

"Hey Blackie, beat it. This is my area."

The voice was a black-brown Rottweiler mix, just down from me. I look around, I see there's all kinds of room, so I ask him. Politely, of course.

"Come on, I just need a little space. You've got plenty of room."

He lumbers over right in my muzzle. He's got a deep white scar on one jowl, the stitches pulled his face sideways until he looks creepy. Drool runs out of out of that side of his mouth and hangs halfway to the floor.

"What'd you say, dog puke?"

I back up as far as I can, trying to stay out of biting range. I don't want to be bit anymore.

"I...I thought there was room for me."

He looks on either side of me. There's enough space for six dogs.

"Well, there isn't. So beat it." He curls his lip and growls.

I jump up and run across the room. There's no where left but next to Major, the alpha dog. I slink into the space next to him and try to look small and harmless. I don't try to look friendly anymore, it just gets you bit.

When I can't stand it anymore, I sneak a peak at the German Shepherd. His coat is scruffy and marked with bare spots and scars, although his muscles still look hard and firm. But it's the way he carries himself I notice. He sits tall, head high, his eyes bright and intelligent.

Now he swings around and looks right at me. I feel insignificant in his presence. I hope he doesn't make me move 'cause there's nowhere else to go.

63

He stares at me a long time, then he speaks.

"Why do you let them do that?"

My mouth falls open, I'm surprised he's talkin' so nice. "Let them do what?"

"Why do you let them push you around?"

I don't know what to say to him, so I just tell the truth. "I don't let them, they just do."

He turns back and looks around the room. "What's your name, pup?"

"Chili," I say proudly.

"Well, Chili. Are you a cat or are you a dog?"

That's a huge insult, but I hold my temper 'cause this is the alpha. "I'm a Black Labrador, but I have some Blue-Tic hound in me."

He seems amused by this. "I can see what you look like, but you act like a cat. No, you act more like a mouse. Even a cat will use his claws when threatened."

"I'm not a coward, I just don't want to get bit." It sounds like a puppy whine and I feel embarrassed the moment I say it.

Major looks at my coat. "But you have bites now, don't you?"

I know they're there, they still hurt. "These bites don't matter. Soon my humans will be back to get me and take me home. They'll patch me up."

When he looks down at me again, his eyes are soft and kind. "Pup, I'm sorry. Your humans aren't coming back."

I flash with anger, then fear. "No! They said they'd be back."

"Yes, but they lied. That's what they say when they don't want to hurt you. That's what they say when they can't face giving you up."

I can't believe that could happen to me. I don't believe him, I don't care if he is the alpha dog.

He asks me, "How long you been here?"

I've got no idea, I've lost all track of time. I stare at the concrete floor, my brain is too confused to remember. "I don't know."

"I know, because I watch. Some dogs come in here and leave soon after. Some never leave. If you're still here after three or four meal-times, your humans are not coming back."

It seems like what I feared most was probably true.

"This is your new life, Chili. Get used to it."

I imagine livin' in this place forever and I'm scared, I don't think I can make it. I hope they come back.

"What about you, Major. How long have you been here?"

"Longer than almost all the dogs. I was like you, at first. I was sure my human would return." He seems angry all of a sudden, his tone is harsh. "Don't let the other dogs push you around. It will only get worse."

"But I'm only a friendly Lab. I'm not big. I'm not mean. I just want to have fun."

If he's disappointed in me he doesn't show it. "You can't change how you look. But you can change how you act. You can choose to be strong and fierce."

I hang my head. "They'll hurt me if I fight them."

"They hurt you now. Besides, there are worse things than pain. Where's your pride? You dishonor yourself when you're weak."

"I'm not weak, I just want to be left alone."

"Do you want to live? Someday a dog will do more than bite you. When that happens, will you be a survivor or a dead coward?"

"I want to live."

"Then remember this. Sometime, somewhere, every dog has to fight or die."

TEN

When we got back from the hike, me and Meatloaf helped Robert wash the Jeep. We let him do the hard parts, we just went under the hose spray and got wet. It really cooled us off. We were due for a bath anyway, we get one once a week whether we need it or not. I think we smell better before the bath, but I don't think Judy does.

We crashed after eating second meal. We almost missed the trip to the park because we were sleeping so good, but Robert woke us up when he opened the drawer with our leashes and collars.

Some of the pack was waiting for us, sniffing the grass. We put our noses down and joined them. We need to smell the grass like Robert needs to read the papers in the morning. It's the same thing, you get all the local news and information.

I looked for Simba, but she wasn't there, I hoped I hadn't missed her. We sniffed, ran around a little, did some personal business, and then got down to neighborhood business with the pack.

"Hey Gizmo, you get home all right this morning?"

"Barely."

"That fence jump was cool," said Roxie. "I think Gizmo could be in the Olympics. Can you do backward flips?"

He nodded. "You should see me with a frisbee. Hey Taser, tell us about the briefcase, what was so important about it?"

I hesitated. "Look, I can't talk about that yet. I got to check it out more, I don't want to be wrong about this."

"What about the plastic thing?"

I stammered, in the panic I'd forgot all about it, the strip was probably still on the ground inside the gate. "Later," I said.

66

"What'd the crime scene look like?" Winston asked. "Was she still in Rigor?"

Roxie and I looked at each other. "Rigor?"

"Rigor mortis. When the body gets stiff like a board. Onset is three to four hours after death, usually lasts seventy-two hours. The Medical Examiner can use it for determining time of death."

This pooch had way too-much free time on his paws, I thought.

"What's an hour?" Meatloaf asked.

I didn't wait for Winston to answer. "Winston, her body was gone. The police were done investigating. They'd come and cleaned up inside the house already."

"No blinkin' blood on the wall or nothing?" He seemed crushed.

"Nothing. Maybe the carpet, I couldn't tell from lookin', her blood smell was everywhere."

"So what's left to investigate?"

I told them about our hike in the hills with Brian today and what I understood about the police findings so far, like only the camera taken.

Gizmo was very interested. "So the police got no idea who could have done it?"

"Nope. They don't have any good evidence, either.

"What about when you went in the house? Didn't you smell a stranger? The killer was inside the house."

I wavered. I didn't want to start any rumors. "There were a lot of different human scents. It's hard to tell how old they were. Besides, smells are only part of the picture. We need evidence."

Winston nodded. "He's spot-on. Smells would be inadmissible in a Court of Law."

"Besides, Gizmo said his humans had been over there for a barbeque," I said. "Their smells are in the house along with everyone else."

"Your humans have been there, too, Taser." added Roxie.

"Right." I'd smelled both Robert and Judy. "So picking up one human's scent or another doesn't prove anything."

"Clues and suspects are good, but we need to think about motive," said Gizmo.

"Means, motive and opportunity," Winston added. "You need all three."

I liked it. Finally we were learning something usable from the Court TV expert.

Winston turned to Gizmo. "Tell us more about these barbeque parties you went to with your humans."

Gizmo shrugged. "What's to tell?"

"What goes on there?"

"They cook stuff on the barbeque oven, sometimes we get some leftover bones. They have beans, dip, different salad bowls—I hate that lettuce stuff, don't you?"

"Are the humans drinking alcohol?"

"Yeah, the males usually drink beer, the females drink wine—like that. Sometimes they have some of that Jose stuff, the stuff in a bottle."

Winston nodded. "Are they swimming?"

"Sure," said Gizmo. "Most of them get in the pool. To cool off, I guess."

"Music? Loud music?"

"Loud, yeah, hurts my ears."

"Right. I've heard it all the way over at my house. Dancing? Any humans dancing?"

"No. No dancing."

"They play games?"

"No, just talk. But they get a little wild sometimes."

"Wild?"

"You know, joking around, teasing, chasing each other. Just like dogs at the park."

"Uh huh. How many couples we talking about?"

"Eight, ten humans."

"Early or late?"

"They start during lighttime and go until darktime. Sometimes I don't get to eat until late, except for scraps from the barbeque."

"OK. I'm beginning to see the setup," Winston said. "Bunch of couples, sitting around the pool all day in wet, skimpy bathing suits, drinking wine coolers and beer, feelin' happy. Then the tequila and lime comes out and everybody's doing shooters and gettin' bladdered. Pretty soon a couple sloshed dollies take off their tops. Then they start with the body shots—"

"Wait." I had to jump in. "Winston, where you gettin' all this?"

"Before you know it, some lad makes a serious pass and they're off for a little rumpy-pumpy."

"Whoa! Whoa. Back off. You're talkin' about our humans here." I couldn't imagine anyone mounting Judy. Even Robert.

"Jealousy. The green-eyed monster. There's real motive for you, dogs. All you gotta do is look at what happens at these parties. It's wild. Male fistfights. Female catfights. Our little suburb is no different than an L.A. suburb."

"I knew it," said Roxie. "He's been watching the Entertainment Channel."

"Hey," Winston objected. "I don't make this stuff up. I'm just giving you a dose of reality. These humans don't have to wait for their season, you know. They're in heat all the time."

Meatloaf had been listening intently. "You know, that's the problem with alcohol. Some humans have anger-management issues that surface after a couple of drinks. That wouldn't happen with seed pods or mushrooms."

Gizmo looked at me funny. "What's he talkin' about, Taser?"

"I'll explain later."

Roxie held up her paw. "I don't want anyone to get the wrong idea, but I saw Bandit's male human go over Nelly's more than once during the day. And Nelly's male wasn't home but her female was."

Gizmo looked excited. "I saw him give her a little piece of paper at a barbeque party one time, like a secret note or something."

I knew this was off. "He's a plumber, he fixed my Robert's sink once. He probably just gave Nelly's female a bill for fixing her sink."

"A plumber." said Meatloaf. "No wonder he drives a German car."

"Let's talk about means," said Roxie.

"Means?"

"First motive." said Gizmo. "If Winston is right and jealousy is the motive, then maybe Nelly's male-human got jealous and killed her for mounting-around."

"That's possible."

"Now 'means' is how she died, the method. Her throat was slashed with a knife. Blood everywhere. What kind of human would do something so horrible to their mate?"

"Precisely, much too messy," Winston said. "Why not use a gun? Very impersonal. Something simple, like a Smith and Wesson thirty-eight revolver."

"My Fresno human had the Revolver album," said Meatloaf. "He played it a lot. He said the Beatles explored new ground with that work."

"A gun?" I said. "Too loud. The neighbors would hear and call the cops."

"What about hitting her on the head?" asked Gizmo. "That's quiet. Messy, maybe—but quiet."

Meatloaf spoke up again. "I been hit with a newspaper, it makes a loud sound. Whack! Right on the butt."

"A crowbar. Silent but deadly."

"Who carries a crowbar? It would be something like a tire iron."

"Or a golf club."

"Everybody around here plays golf."

The pack nodded.

"We're getting' off track here," I said. "Police said she was killed with a knife. I think it was done by an unknown intruder, somebody who came over their fence from the desert. It couldn't be Nelly's male human, he wasn't even home, he was traveling for work."

70

Winston agreed. "Nelly's male didn't have opportunity."

"But Taser heard nothing was stolen from the house besides a camera. So what's the motive?"

"Wait a minute. Look who's coming," Roxie said.

It was Bandit. He trotted right over to the pack like nothin' was wrong.

I was still ticked about this morning, seeing Bandit only made me madder. "Hey big mouth. What's with blowin' our cover this morning?"

He stood his ground, flexing his haunches for all to see. "Just protecting my neighborhood from burglars and thieves. That's what dogs are supposed to do, aren't they? Bark at burglars?"

"You wouldn't know a burglar if he bit you on your butt," I said.

He stepped toward me, muscles flexed. "Is that a threat, Basset ears?"

Gizmo raised a paw. "Hey, dogs, cool it. We all want the same thing. We're just looking out for our masters."

The hairs on my back started to rise. "I don't think so. I think bonebreath here is lookin' out for himself. He wants our investigation to fail. I don't think we shouldn't say anything more in front of him."

Meatloaf jumped in theg argument. "Yeah Bandit, you weren't such a hot watchdog when Nelly's human got murdered right next door to you."

Bandit spun around and got in Meatloaf's muzzle. "Shut up, you old fool. Why don't you go over in the corner and lick yourself."

That was it. Nobody disses my partner.

Bandit was sideways to me now. I launched myself low and hard at his left flank. His rear legs lost their footing and he landed clumsily on his rear. Before he could get his paws under him, I hit him again in the chest. He bit me hard on my muzzle on his way down. The pack jumped back out of the way and the fight was on.

Bandit landed on his back. I leaped on him instantly and locked my jaws on his throat. I held him there while his legs kicked at the sky, my

71

own loud growls muffling his whining protest. The harder I bit, the more he whined.

I vaguely heard Meatloaf speaking through the fog.

"Taser, that's enough."

I bit harder.

"Taser! No more, dawg."

Something primal came over me, I wasn't gonna let loose of Bandit until this thing was finished. I squeezed and growled louder.

That's when a human hand grabbed my collar.

TASER, NO!

It was Robert. I released my jaws and got up.

No fighting.

I stepped back. Bandit rolled over and got up coughing. His female-human looked him over while Robert talked to her. It looked like Bandit was all right, he shook his head and hacked a bit. He'd live. I left marks but hadn't broken his skin.

Robert put me on a leash and kept me close. Bandit's female-human put him on his leash and brought him over to me until Bandit and I stood nose to nose. I resisted the urge to bite him again.

Now make up and be nice, she said.

She held him in front of me, like I was supposed to say I was sorry or something.

Tell your friend you're sorry.

This human was a real bonehead.

I looked Bandit in the eye. "Mount you, buttsniffer."

"I'll get you for this," he spit back.

Then the human led Bandit out of the park and back to their house. The pack gathered around me in a show of support.

Meatloaf checked out my wound. "You all right, dawg?"

I shook off the pain. "I been bit harder by bitches."

Winston did a little Bulldog dance sideways. "Now that was a bloody dogfight!"

***

When we got back to the house, Robert put some stuff from a tube on my muzzle and it felt better right away. I wasn't sorry about jumping on Bandit, and for some reason Robert didn't seem to care either. Judy ignored it too, probably because she was disgusted with us. The rest of the evening was pretty normal, we didn't hear any yelling or arguing.

We lay on the floor while our humans watched television. Meatloaf was soon snoring, but I couldn't sleep. I was still wound-up from the dog fight, but something else bothered me. I was trying to understand Bandit's problem with investigating this murder. Roxie said Bandit's master had visited Nelly's place. Maybe Bandit knew more about what happened that night than he was telling us. Maybe he was keeping quiet for a reason.

Then I remembered the briefcase smell and it complicated the whole mess. That's why I couldn't think about it, it was too upsetting. I thought I should just quit worrying about it, it was a human problem and we were just dogs.

But meddling was in our genes. Dogs that didn't manipulate humans to better their condition didn't survive. We're doing so well as a species because we have our humans for close allies. They feed us because we take care of them, love them, protect them from threats. It's what we do.

It's what they expect.

I got up and wandered outside. The wind was blowing again, it smelled more like rain now than in a long time. Lighting flashed far away as dried twigs and leaves tumbled across the patio. I stuck my nose in the dog house and sniffed the briefcase. I could still smell the problem, faintly. Sometimes I could smell it, sometimes I couldn't. It was so faint I almost doubted it was there. If it was possible to imagine a scent, I guess this could be one of those.

I finally remembered that stupid plastic strip Gizmo dropped. I trotted to the gate and sniffed around until I found it in the gravel. I grabbed it and dropped it in the dog house next to the briefcase, I'd have to deal with it later when things calmed down.

I went out to the yard and watched the lighting. It didn't scare me, neither did thunder. I had other fears tonight.

When Robert started turning off lights I went inside to get my bone. Meatloaf left his for me and went to bed, he said he was too exhausted from the hike. I took both bones outside and dropped them through the fence.

Tonight I decided to confront the coyote. I left her bones in the usual place, then backed up five dog lengths and sat tall, so she could see me. The night-light was up now and it was bright enough for her to see me sitting there waiting. I knew she'd pick up my scent well before that.

I saw her flit between the creosote bushes far out there. She moved with purpose, like she knew just where she was goin' and didn't have time to waste. When she got within a ball's throw, she stopped and looked right at me. She waited a moment, then slowly walked closer.

I don't know why I waited tonight, I think I needed to know more about her breed. I wanted to know how they survived without human help, how they found their own food and water. I was jealous of their freedom.

When she was close to the fence I could see her clearly. She was as skinny as a creature could be, barely thirty pounds but about my height. Her ears stood straight up and out, forming two tips of the triangle completed by her pointed snout. Her eyes were glowing yellow slits that offered neither warmth nor trust.

She stopped right at the fence line. I jumped right in before she ran away.

"What is your name?" I asked her.

She stared but didn't speak. There wasn't a trace of fear.

"Please, your name," I repeated.

"Dominga."

74

My head jerked back at the sound of her voice, I wasn't expecting her to answer. She sounded like a dog, but with a strange accent.

"Why do you leave this food?" She demanded.

"We have all we need. We have more than we need. I wanted to help."

She moved closer.

"Do you have pups?"

She didn't seem to understand.

"Do you have small ones?" I tried.

"I have two that lived. They are always hungry."

"What about a mate, their father? Does anyone help you?"

"Coyotes help themselves. It is our way. We have no one but ourselves."

She bent to take the bones.

"Wait." I had a sudden thought. "Are you out there every night, close to us?"

She hesitated before answering. "I am."

"Some days ago, did you hear one of us, a dog who lives down from here, howling at night?'

"I heard two howls from your kind."

"Yes! Yes, that was it. Did you see anything? Before the howl? I think a human jumped over the fence at the house, just before."

She looked at me with distrust. "Why should I tell you this?"

"Because he was a bad human."

She sniffed. "All humans are bad."

"This human was the worst kind," I said.

"An outlaw?"

"Yes, an outlaw."

She lifted her head. "I am an outlaw, too. You expect me to hurt a brother? Maybe this human was hungry."

"No, no. This human killed one of his own, a female-human."

She paused. "We kill."

Neither proud nor ashamed. Just fact.

75

"But you don't kill other coyotes. This killing was different."

She looked left and right. "I do not care if humans die. We would eat them for food if we could."

"Coyotes kill for food, I understand that, that's all right."

She snorted. "All right? We do not need your permission to hunt. We kill for food as you would kill, if you were not fat and spoiled. Look at you."

Suddenly I felt much too domesticated. I hoped she hadn't got a good look at Meatloaf.

"Your humans take this land with their machines. They run off our prey. We cannot feed our families because you leave us only scraps."

"I'm sorry. But I can't change that."

"When we come for your fat rabbits, they chase us and call us outlaws on our own land. No! Humans are the outlaws. This is our land. I was born here as my mother was born here."

"Dominga, please. This human is different. He did not kill for food, I believe he's evil."

She seemed to consider this. "I know what you speak. I have seen evil."

She spoke with some sympathy this time.

"Can you help me?" I asked.

"What is your name, fat one?"

"Taser."

Dominga stared at me for a long time, then said, "I must feed my small ones."

She picked up the bones and ran off into the night.

ELEVEN

I don't know what happened, but I think it was my fault. Robert was talking loud and using those funny words he only uses when he's mad. But he wasn't mad at us and he wasn't mad at Judy so I couldn't figure it out.

It started when he went out to get the news papers first thing in the morning. Meatloaf and I were tired from the hike, so we were still asleep and didn't hear him come down. Robert went outside, then came back in and looked in the garage, then he went back outside. I followed him out the second time.

He talked to me and pointed at the driveway, but I couldn't see anything. Then I heard the word Jeep and I knew. We'd left the Jeep in the driveway after we washed it. This morning it was gone.

Robert said more funny words. He was not happy.

I felt terrible, mostly because last night I had one of those bad dreams. I heard a truck motor running and I saw truck headlights and I heard Zeus' name. But I know now it must have been the Jeep motor and the Jeep headlights. I didn't do my job. I didn't protect my human. Nothing could be done now, so I went in and lay down next to Meatloaf, feeling sadder than I had in a long time.

I heard Robert get on the phone to the police. They talked a while, then he finally got around to feeding us first-meal. We were pretty hungry by then. After that Judy made some bacon and eggs and toast. Bacon's gotta be my favorite smell in the whole world. I love when they cook this food. I think it's because if you stick around the kitchen after they eat, sometimes a piece of bacon just falls from the sky and lands in front of your nose.

Some time later a police-human came to the door, but we didn't bark because we knew we were in trouble for sleeping on the job. He talked to Robert about numbers and locks and stuff I don't know anything about, and he wrote on a lot of papers. Then he left.

I wondered if this meant we wouldn't go on any desert hikes anymore. I don't know why we couldn't take Judy's car. She's got a Volvo, I think. They're supposed to be tough, it could handle those desert roads. Maybe she didn't let him drive it without her along to talk at him.

Then he and Judy changed into some nice clothes and got in her little car and left. Meatloaf heard them talking but I missed it 'cause I was out in the yard peein' on a tree. Believe me when I tell you, these desert trees are hard to hit. They're so skinny it takes good aim and lots of practice. When I was done, I went back inside to check with my partner.

"Meat, what'd they say?"

He shook his head. "They're going to Phoenix to look at city apartments."

"What? Why?"

"Robert's mad. He wants to sell the house now and move."

"Because somebody stole his Jeep? He can get a new Jeep."

"He says the neighborhood is going to the dogs. What do you suppose that means?"

"I don't know, but I wouldn't take it personal."

This was a catastrophe. If we got dumped at the pound we may never get out. I might get another human, but Meatloaf was old, and he had that gimp shoulder. Nobody would take him. I don't think he knew how serious this was.

"Meatloaf, we really gotta solve this case."

"You mean now we have to find a Jeep-thief?"

"No, we gotta find the killer."

"What more can we do? We got the whole pack working on it."

"Come outside with me a minute, out back."

He peeled himself off the carpet and followed me out the dog door. I trotted over to our dog house and motioned inside with my nose.

"You see that briefcase?"

Meatloaf peeked in. "Of course, my eyes aren't that bad."

"Go in there and smell it."

"You know I hate this dog house."

"What's your problem?"

"It's not natural materials."

"The dog house? It's just plastic, go on in."

"I'm not going in there. Plastic isn't natural."

"They make it from oil. Oil comes from the ground, that's as natural as your seed pod tree."

"It's a man-made product, depleting our planet's natural resources. And it makes you dumb just smelling it."

"Meatloaf, you eat plastic. Would you just go in and sniff?"

He looked in again and shivered. "There's probably roaches in there."

"There's no roaches. I been in there. The bug-human came and sprayed not too long ago, remember?"

"I hate those big ones we get in the hot time."

"Trust me."

Meatloaf poked his head in.

"Go on, smell the briefcase. Smell it good."

"What is it?"

"I don't want to put the scent in your nose. You tell me what it is."

He went in and sniffed it all over. "I smell Nelly's male, no surprise there. Mostly I smell leather, cow leather. Leather with some kind of dye. Then there's computer paper and paper-ink smell, a laser printer. Some photographs in color. Plastic something and metal stuff, maybe it's the lock on the briefcase. And chewing gum, spearmint flavor, Wrigleys. He had a ham sandwich in there not long ago. On whole wheat with mustard. Dijon mustard."

He sniffed some more.

"Coffee, of course. He spilled his coffee on it. Half-decaf, cream, no sugar. He carries his newspaper in there. The New York one like Judy reads. I smell drycleaning fluid, he must carry this briefcase when he wears his nice clothes. And I think he set it on a counter recently that had some chocolate chip ice cream on it." He sniffed once more. "Dreyers."

He beamed at me, pleased with himself. "That what you got?"

I hated to tell him. "You're right about everything but the ice cream. It's Ben and Jerry's brand, Chocolate-Chip Cookie Dough"

"That's the special smell?"

"No. I'm not surprised that you missed it. Sometimes I can't pick it up, either. I smell something else, but I think it's in a plastic bag. "

"A baggie?"

"Not drugs. I'm not sure yet. So tell me, you think those papers are Judy's?"

"No, Taser. It's the New York papers like she reads. Same ink."

"Yeah, you're right."

"Why don't you open it up and look inside?"

"I'm all toes, for one thing. Have you seen that buckle and latch?"

Meatloaf looked it over. "Looks tough. You want me to chew a hole in the bottom?"

"As thick as it is, it may take you days. Besides, you might destroy the plastic bag while you're at it. Bad chain of evidence. We're kinda stuck."

"Wait a minute. What's that white thing on the floor?"

I looked inside the doghouse. "Oh yeah, that plastic strip thing, I got it from Nelly's place. It smells important, but I haven't had time to figure it out."

Meatloaf went in the dog house and stared down at it. "You know what this thing is?"

"No idea."

"It's a test strip. My humans in Fresno used 'em. I ate a whole box one day and OD'd."

"Odeed?"

"Overdosed," he said. "It was a bad trip, believe me. They took me to the Vet hospital. I can still remember puking."

"Bad trip to the vet?"

"See, my humans were trying to have a pup, so she always had these things around. I got the box off her bathroom sink. My male explained it to me later." He pointed one paw at the plastic strip. "One line, no litter. Two lines, you're gonna have a litter."

"What's this one?" I asked.

"It's got two lines. This is Vicki's odor, right?"

"Yeah. Smells that way to me."

"She's with-pup. Or she was, anyway, before she was murdered."

This changed things. Humans always acted weird when pups were coming. "This is important, partner. I'm not sure just what it means."

"Maybe the pack has some ideas."

"We'll check. But don't talk about the briefcase yet, OK?"

"You da pooch."

"Thanks Meatloaf. I'm goin' upstairs for a quick look while they're gone."

He followed me back in the house. "Whatever, dawg. Be careful."

He didn't have to warn me, I didn't want to get caught upstairs myself. That's as bad as playing underpants tug-a-war when they're sitting on the big white water dish.

I ran up the stairs and went through their room. Not much had changed in the bedroom or their bathroom. Judy's counter was clean and Robert's was a mess. I dashed to Robert's hobby room and looked out the window. No one seemed at home at Nelly's, certainly no one had been cleaning up. The swimming pool looked even dirtier and darker. The little tree in their backyard seemed worse, now its leaves were falling off. If I only knew all about plants like Victor did. Robert said the guy had a green thumb, but I couldn't tell if that was true or not.

Then I remembered something.

I jogged downstairs, went in the family room and stepped on the TV changer until the television blinked on. Gizmo said something about the Garden Channel, I think. I kept flipping until I saw plants and stuff. Then I sat down and watched.

If it took a green paw to solve this problem, I was willing to get one.

***

By the time Robert and Judy got home, I'd seen Working with Bamboo, Planning your Garden, Hot Weather Plants, and Hardscaping Ideas. None of it helped me, I'd need to watch more of this channel later.

Robert and Judy went upstairs a while to make the bed or somethin', so me and Meatloaf took a nap. It was a lazy afternoon and we needed our rest anyway. We were pretty tired, so we slept until dinner, but perked up on the way to the park at dusk. Somethin' was always happening at the park and you can't beat the smells. We pulled on the leash all the way there.

Before we hit the grass, I saw the pack sniffing a new dog with spiky ears. It looked like an older Doberman Pinscher. His muscles were soft and he had some white hair on his muzzle.

Gizmo introduced him. "This is Spike, he lives couple streets over."

I nodded at him. "Name's Taser." We sniffed each other, and I picked up a definite hint of garlic and Italian sausage. "My buddy here is Meatloaf."

He acknowledged my partner, then looked around. "Nice park you got here. We got nuttin like dis in Cottonwood."

Right.

"No, but at least you've got more trees than we do."

He looked at me funny. "Trees?"

"Yeah. Cottonwood trees. Tall, grey leaves, white bark?"

"Oh yeah."

"It's cooler in Cottonwood, too. I bet you miss that part."

Spike looked down. "Yeah, I miss da snow."

Gizmo jumped in. "We been a little upset lately, one of our friends lost her human."

Spike didn't seem concerned. "Dat right."

"Vicki, a female murdered in her own bed," I said. "Few nights ago, right down the street here."

"Sorry. So, they catch the perp?"

"No." Winston stuck his snout in. "We think she was hit."

Spike cocked his head. "She got hit wit a car?"

"No," Winston said. "Snuffed. Capped. Rubbed out. You know, whacked."

Spike backed up a little. "Ya know, I better be goin'. Pleased to meet you." Then he ran off to his human waiting down the street for him.

I turned to Winston. "That was subtle. Whacked? Snuffed? Why didn't you just come out and accuse his master?"

"Did you see him take off when I threw the lingo at him? I'm telling you, they're as bent as a bottle of chips. We need to keep an eye on those two."

"Spike says he misses the snow? Who misses snow?" Roxie said.

"I don't think it snows in Cottonwood," added Gizmo.

Winston seemed doubtful too. "He looked down and to the left when he answered. That's a sure sign someone's lying. Besides, this H.O.A. thing looks bad for him."

I cocked my head. "H.O.A.? I miss somethin' here?"

Roxie apologized. "Sorry, you weren't here. I heard my humans talking at first-meal. They said they saw an argument at the letterboxes between Vicki and Spike's male."

"You're kidding. When?" I asked.

"Some time before the murder. I guess Vicki called the H.O.A. on our hitman for working on his car in the front yard. Apparently he got oil on the driveway."

"Oil on the concrete? No way."

"Unbelievable."

Meatloaf cocked his head. "What's an H.O.A.?"

"Home Owner's Association." I said. "They're like the Mafia, but meaner. You never want to get on their bad side."

"Yeah," said Gizmo. "I've seen the look on my human's face when he got one of those violation letters from the HOA people. You'd think someone had just run over his dog."

"Do the police-humans know this?" I asked.

"Dunno."

I wasn't too sure about their take on this hitman. "What happened to your jealous mate theory, Winston? I been thinking about Bandit's male-human going over there during the day. Maybe that's why Bandit doesn't want us investigating."

Meatloaf nudged me with his snout. "Tell 'em"

I glanced around at each face, pausing for impact. "Vicki. She was with-pup."

"No!"

I told them how Gizmo and I took the plastic test strip, and how Meatloaf knew what it meant.

"Crikey. This changes everything," said Winston. "Suppose it wasn't her mate's pup. Maybe some neighbor mounted her and a pup wasn't supposed to happen."

Roxie knew what that would mean. "And Victor got jealous, jealous enough to get rid of her."

Meatloaf was confused. "So Victor murdered Vicki? He killed his own mate?"

"I don't think so," Gizmo said. "I think a neighbor murdered Vicki to keep it quiet. He wouldn't want anyone to know they were mounting-around. Nobody likes their mates mounting-around. They take the big-screen TV and move out."

Winston jumped up and down. "Gizmo! I like your thinking. But we need to clarify our terminology to avoid confusion. The one doing the mounting is called the Mount-er. The one being mounted is called the Mount-ee."

I understood. "Gizmo thinks the Mount-er wasn't the Mount-ee's official mate."

"Any of the neighborhood males at these parties could be the Mount-er. It could've been more than one male."

"I told you," said Winston. "This is one hot human. She's got her own motorcycle, did you know? One of those bright-yellow Italian jobs with the loud pipes. She rides around in these tight leather pants looking like some kind of pro skirt."

"I don't know, I'm backing the jealous mate theory," said Roxie. "No one wants to raise someone else's pup. I think it was Victor who murdered her."

"Maybe, maybe not," I said. "I think Gizmo could be right. That's why Bandit doesn't like this investigation. It might be his male-human, the plumber."

"Yeah," said Meatloaf. "Plumbers mount everyone. It's what they do."

I nodded.

"Here comes Simba, let's ask what she thinks about Vicki," said Winston.

We turned to look. Simba got to the park, barked twice at us and went for a run on the grass.

"I'll go ask," I said. Then I chased after her, happy to get her alone.

I saw her look back at me. She stopped to wait, then took off as soon as I got close. She was fast. I finally caught her at the far end of the park and gave her a bump with my hip. She tumbled and I stumbled, I ended up half on top of her. She gave me a nip on my ear with her sharp teeth.

I love when they do that.

She smelled clean but musky, like a real dog. Her hair was long and soft, softer than any Labrador I'd ever been with. She sniffed my face closely and looked concerned.

"What happened to your muzzle?" she asked.

"Nothin' serious. I got into it with Bandit last night, he made fun of Meatloaf."

"My, you're quite the animal, aren't you?"

I couldn't tell if that was good or bad. "I need to talk to you."

"Sure, what's up?"

I glanced back at the pack. "Winston came up with this theory about Nelly's female and those wild parties they had. We think Vicki let other humans mount her—other humans besides her mate. They think she was in heat all the time."

She looked slightly amused. "Well. I see where the conversation goes when I'm not here."

I was a little embarrassed by the subject. "Does it seem likely she could be that way?"

"All I know is what my humans said. We used to go to those parties until they got too wild. They said Nelly's female really threw it around. I saw some of it."

"Threw it around?"

"Her female appeal. Like she would receive anyone, anytime. I guess in-heat all the time is the right way to say it."

"Did you ever notice who she was friendly with? Which male?"

"She played around with Bandit's male. Teasing, talking a lot. Robert too."

I choked. "Robert? My Robert?"

"Sure. I saw him throw her in the pool once. Then he jumped in after her. They were acting silly from drinking too much."

This surprised me, Robert always seemed so controlled and calm. It must have been the alcohol drink. "By the way," I said. "Vicki was with-pup."

Simba was shocked. "Nobody has said that before."

I told her about the test strip.

"A detective-dog, too. Very impressive."

Before I could answer, she nipped me again and jumped up.

"We better go back. The others will get suspicious."

86

When we got back over to where the pack was standing, I saw Bandit was there with Remi. Neither of them looked at me, but Bandit spoke directly to Simba.

"Hey, Simba. Missed you last night."

She nodded politely. "We came early, my humans went out last night." She turned to the pack. "I wanted to ask, has anyone seen Buffy?"

Gizmo had seen her. "She was here earlier for a few minutes and left. She said she didn't like sweating."

I looked over and saw Bandit's human watching me, but I couldn't let a chance to insult the weasely Weimaraner go by. "Hey buttsniffer, how's the throat tonight? Wanna go round two?"

He ignored me and turned to Remi. "Remi, I've got some hot news. Have you heard who had their family car stolen last night?"

"No," Remi deadpanned. "Do tell."

"Taser and Meatloaf. Apparently they fell asleep on the job and someone stole their Jeep from out front. Took it right out from under old super-nose."

Remi sniggered like the wuss that he was. "Some detectives. They can't even protect their own house, much less the neighborhood."

Gizmo looked at me in surprise. "That true, Taser?"

I nodded. There was nothing to say.

Bandit kept it up. "You'd think a mutt with ears that big would have heard something."

Now they both laughed.

"Yeah, yeah," I said. "It's true. I slept through it all." I was too embarrassed to look at Simba's reaction.

"Bad break," said Roxie.

"Hey, Remi," said Bandit, "You think it might have been the neighborhood—MURDER-HUMAN?"

Howls of laughter.

That was all I could take. "Ahh, I think I hear my human calling. We'll see you all later."

87

Meatloaf and I beat a retreat, they were still making fun of us as we left. We went up to Robert and tugged on his pants. It was time to get out of there.

That's how life is. Sometimes you get the pooch, sometimes the pooch gets you.

***

I decided to wait to for Dominga again.

I needed to talk with someone, no matter what specie they were. I was feeling like old Mother Hubbard's hound tonight. Meatloaf wasn't upset at all, stuff like this just rolls off his back. Me, I was a little ticked off. I looked up at the sky, but it was black except for the citylight glow from Phoenix. There was no sign of the night-light yet.

She was late.

I started worrying about all the things that could go bad for a wild coyote in a human world and the list was long. In our neighborhood, most humans steered clear of them. Our humans treated coyotes like big skinny rabbits, just part of the local wildlife. Others would like to have 'em removed or killed. Coyotes weren't a protected species around here. Dominga could've been hit by a car when she crossed a road. Her pups would be waiting for her, starving. Even the small chance of it upset me.

Then I saw her pop out of the brush. She didn't slow this time, she trotted right up to the fence and waited for me to speak.

"I brought you another bone, I hope it helps your family."

She didn't respond, other than a slow nod. She seemed wary tonight, like she knew I was gonna ask her more questions. I tried small talk.

"How is the hunting in your desert?"

"Our hunting suffers with the heat. Our rabbits have gone to live near your houses, to get your water and green plants."

"Rain will come soon, like the end of every hot-time."

She didn't answer, so I got to the point.

"Can you tell me any more about the night with the howls? About the human you saw?"

"No. Nothing has changed for us outlaws."

She didn't move or try to leave, that was a hopeful sign.

I tried a different path. "Last night, you said you had seen evil."

"I have."

"Can you tell me about it? How do you know it when you see it?"

She looked to either side. "You will know in your heart."

"Will I see it with my eyes?"

"No. But you can smell it."

That didn't make any sense. "Smell it? How can I smell it?"

"When you smell now, how do you know what you smell? You cannot see it or hear it. But you know what it is."

"Yes."

"You believe your nose more than your eyes, more than your ears."

That was true. "Yes."

"Then you must trust your nose."

That didn't help me with my problem. It was a smell and my nose that got me into this mess. "Dominga, please. I need to know what evil is. Is it like death?"

"No. Death is the escape. Evil is a curse on the living."

"Tell me about this curse."

She thought before she spoke. "Your kind is like us, you should know this. You feel this-day but you also feel next-day, yes?"

I didn't understand. "I don't know what you mean."

"You live now but you want to live more, next-day."

"Yes."

"You dream of better than this day. You believe next-day will be better."

"Yes."

"And even if things are not good next-day, even if all is bad, you do not stop this feeling."

"Yes. We believe this."

89

"What does your kind call this feeling? This belief?" she asked.

I didn't know—unless—yes, I did know. "We call it hope."

"Hope?"

"That's right, we dogs have hope."

"Then know this. Evil lives when hope dies. Evil is the death of all hope in your heart."

Finally, I knew exactly what evil was.

TWELVE

City of Phoenix Dog Pound

Clang!

As I leave my cage, I'm surprised I'm happy to get out in the yard. I seem to have figured out how to get along in the pound, I think it's mostly attitude. It doesn't hurt that everybody sees I'm friends with Major now, they're all leaving me alone. Even my bites have cleared up and there's no new ones.

Every day Major gives me a tip or two on survival or some information about the human world. I know who the good guards are and who the bad guards are in here, and I know how to avoid them. Major's old, but he knows a lot.

After I do my morning business, I drop by to see the big dog. He's at his usual place on the wall, watching over the pound.

"Sleep good, Major?" I asked him.

He shrugged. "As well as you can with this racket."

I don't say nothin' but the noise don't bother me now. I sleep like a dead dog. We sit in silence for a while, watching the crazy ones wander around and bark. Mad Marmaduke is chasing his tail, round and around and around. I never understood that, can't these mutts figure it out?

"Still thinking of Mike and Sandy, pup?" Major asks me out of the blue.

I'm surprised by my answer. "I haven't thought much about them lately. But I still love them."

He nods but looks like he's thinking of something. I'd never had the nerve to ask about his family before, but today I do.

91

"Who was your human, Major?"

Major speaks softly. "My human was young. I belonged to his father, a police-human. He was a good man."

"You were a police dog?"

"No, just a policeman's pet. One day my human died at work, so I went to live with his son. It was good for a while, but then he got married. His wife didn't like dogs." Major looked away. "He said he'd be back, too."

A couple dogs are playing around in front of us, just having fun, when a fuzzy Terrier jumps back and bumps into Major. Our alpha gives the Terrier a stern look, so this dog rolls over on his back in front of Major and submits. Then he leaps up and runs away. I gain even more respect for this gentle alpha.

After I hear Major's story, I start thinkin' about Mike and Sandy leavin' me here and I get a little angry. It doesn't seem right, it doesn't seem fair.

"Major. How come we have to depend on these humans so much? Why can't we make it on our own?"

Major scratched behind his ear. "It was decided long ago, when our fathers came out of the forest to share human fire and food. We traded freedom for security. We're the only species that depends entirely on another species for our survival."

I didn't like that. "I like the love we get, but I don't like the rules. I wanna live my own life."

He looked thoughtful. "You can do both. There are tricks to living with humans."

"I don't like doing tricks."

"Not human dog-tricks, Chili. I mean there are ways to be independent. Do you know human words? Do you listen when they talk?"

I really hadn't listened much, 'cause they usually told me not to do something I wanted to do. "Sometimes. I listen if they say something I want to hear, or if I'm hungry or need to go outside."

"You need to do more than that. I can see you're smart, you could learn their words. Listen when they talk, they say the same words over and over. Don't just play when they're around. And listen to their television words. There are lots of things to learn from the television."

I decide if I ever get out of this place, I'd try it. I don't wanna depend on someone else for the rest of my life.

Then I see Major panting and I worry he may be sick. "You all right?"

"I'm just hot. Aren't you hot in here?"

I look at his coat, he's got all that thick German Shepherd hair. "Yeah, me too," I say, but I'm not really hot at all. I've already shed a bunch.

"I'm so tired of this heat. I've been hot as long as I can remember. I just want to be cool before I die."

Suddenly, I'm more worried about him than myself. "Maybe someone will take you home yet. You still got good years left in you."

He doesn't look at me. "I'm too old. They all want young ones like you. You might get a new human, but I won't. I'm gonna die in this stinking Pound yet."

I don't like him talking like that. "Don't give up, there's always a chance. If you don't have hope, you got nothing left to live for."

He starts to speak, but stops when the dogs up front go wild. They're barking frantically and throwing themselves on their cage walls. It sounds like the barking when they bring in a new dog, but even crazier.

I strain to see, but can't make out anything. "Major, what's happening?"

His voice is different now.

"Rusty was right."

"Rusty? Who's Rusty?"

"One of the Sheriff's drug-sniffing dogs. He said they're bringing the beast over here from the County cage. The one they got in that drug-dealer bust."

Major's got his eyes glued to the front, but I still can't see anything.

"Who they bringin' in?"

"A pro. A Pitbull, bred for professional dog fighting. The kind they beat to make mean. They build 'em up, run 'em on treadmills. Make 'em hang from a stick with their mouth to strengthen their jaws. He's dangerous. He's killed more dogs than we have in this room."

"Why'd they bring him here?"

"The SPCA won't let the County put him to sleep. It got to be a big battle, made all the papers."

Now the barking out front quiets down.

"There's nowhere else to put him. They think he's harmless, but I know better. He lost an eye in his last fight and they neutered him to calm him down. They say he deserves a second chance."

Suddenly, all the barking stops.

Every mutt in the yard stares at the entry hall.

All I can hear is panting as a massive Pitbull steps slowly into the room. He's bigger than most of his kind, at least 110 pounds of muscle. His short neck is as wide as his head, and his head is enormous. He's got scars all over his black muzzle. One eye is dead white, but the other cold, black eye looks around the room at every animal.

Each dog melts under his piercing glare, even the Akita and the Rottweiler mix. One by one the dogs lining the wall turn their eyes. All of them.

Except Major.

The Pitbull locks eyes with our Alpha, then walks directly toward him. Only now do I see the blaze of white hair on his chest. It looks like a star. It looks like...

"Major! What's this dog's name?"

Major doesn't take his eyes off the advancing mass, it's almost across the room.

94

I ask him again, and the moment he answers, I lose the last good feeling I have, the one belief that's kept me moving and breathing in this horrible place.

I lose all hope.

"His name," Major says, "is Zeus."

THIRTEEN

I hit the Garden Channel right after Robert left for work. I'd already seen "How to Build a Deck", "Making Cheap Planters", and now I was into "Garden Plants for Color". At this rate, I figured I'd have a white muzzle before I got a green paw. What I needed was a TV show on manure. Maybe the Golf Channel would be a better choice, they seem to have all these huge grass parks. But I've never see any dogs in their parks, so maybe the stuff they used for manure had dog repellant in it, somethin' like that bitter spray Judy uses to keep us from eating the kitchen table legs. Seems like a waste of good grass to me.

Judy came down before first-meal with her suitcase bags and left before Robert got up, so I guessed it's gonna be just males in the house for a while. That suit me fine, that meant the lid would be up on the big white water. We like those better than our little bowls, 'cause the water's cooler in the big white dish.

We hadn't heard any more of that nonsense about selling our house, so maybe that all blew over. Still, I'm not taking any chances. I gotta find this murder-human yet. I thought I better tell my partner about the briefcase smell and get his opinion.

Meatloaf was doin' somethin' in the kitchen, I heard him messin' around in there, so I checked it out. I'd had enough of the Garden Channel. When I walked in the kitchen, he had this white package in his mouth and was just standin' there stupid. He looked like he'd been caught leavin' a pile on the rug.

"Meatloaf? What's that?"

"Hhhh. Hhhhhhhh. Hhh."

I can't understand him 'cause of that thing in his mouth. He took it through the dog door and ran out in the bushes with it. I ran after him and watched him drop the package on the ground.

Catcrap!

It was a package of steak.

"Meatloaf! That's major dog felony. What're you thinking?"

He shrugged his shoulders. "Mount 'em. They're gonna dump us at the pound anyway, what do we care if they yell at us now?"

I sniffed it close, it didn't smell like steak very much to me. So I put my paw on top and felt it. "Frozen?"

Meatloaf nodded. "Robert left it on the counter to thaw. Don't worry, he probably won't figure it out. I use to do this to my human in Fresno."

"Do what?"

"These humans don't think very good in the morning. They put something out on the counter to thaw and then go to work. When they come home and don't see it, they think they forgot to take it out."

"What about the package?"

"And you gotta be careful not to eat any of the white stuff, because it comes out later in your poop and you're busted. I usually bury the white stuff."

Meatloaf wasn't as dumb as he acted.

"When can we eat it?" I asked.

"It's not for us. I thought we'd give it to Dominga, she needs it worse than we do. It'll be soft after our second-meal."

"Smart dog. Why don't you bury it while I go upstairs and sniff around."

"I'm on it."

I trotted up the stairs and went right to the little hobby room and its window. I nosed the curtains aside and looked out at the murder house. It didn't look like Victor or any other human had been back, the place was lookin' pretty shabby. The pool looked dark and filthy, and the grass out front needed shortening. That little tree in back looked dead, its leaves had fallen off. I figured Victor must be plenty upset to let things go like that.

Then I decided to do more investigating. Trust your nose, Dominga said.

I started sniffing in the hobby room closet first. Robert had boxes with paper and ink smell stacked in there. I nosed each one.

Nothin'.

There were a few boxes with metal tool odor, and some boxes with stinky glue like he uses on the little airplanes. His work bench had two drawers. I nosed the bottom one, then the top, then went back to the bottom. Somethin' was in there that smelled like Vickie. I pulled on it, but it was hard to move. I bit harder on the knob and gave a tug. It slid open halfway.

There were some thin books, a key ring, a couple small tools and some papers inside. The key ring had one key on it. Sniff sniff. I bit the plastic piece on the ring and took it out. Sniff. I thought I had something, but I knew I had to check with Meatloaf to make sure. I put my butt against the drawer and pushed it shut.

I carried the key ring to the top of the stairs and left it, then went to check out Robert and Judy's bedroom.

They had a small television on a table against one wall. I went over and put my nose against the biggest button I could see. The TV flashed on, and when the picture came up I checked what channel they were watching. It was the news-head station. That was kinda interesting. He watches boring news-humans with his mate, but he throws neighbor Vicki in the pool and jumps in after her.

Maybe Judy is the Yellow Lab sister-type while Vicki was the exotic Golden Retriever.

I needed to talk to Meatloaf about this. I picked up the key ring and ran down the stairs, he was just coming in the dog door.

"All set," he said. "I buried it right behind the bush where we talk to Dominga."

Then he saw the key ring hanging from my teeth.

"Whazzat?"

I spat it out on the kitchen floor. "I think it's a key to Nelly's house. Whadda ya think?"

Meatloaf came over and put his nose very close. The trick when you sniff like a dog is to get your nose really, really, close—but not touch it. If you're gonna sniff some other dog's business, you learn that skill real early in life.

He seemed satisfied with his inspection. "Smells like the Vicki female to me. Where'd you get it?"

"Out of a drawer in Robert's airplane room. It was with his personal stuff."

"You don't know if it's a house key." Meatloaf sniffed it again. "Maybe it's a car key."

I shook my muzzle. "I know what a house key looks like. The car keys have that plastic lump on them. I ate a car key once, the plastic part, anyway."

"So he's got a key to her house. Big deal."

"Let me ask you somethin'. You think Robert mounts Judy? I mean they're mates, that's what mates do sometimes."

"Yeah, I know he does," Meatloaf said. "He did it yesterday after they went to see city-apartments. My nose told me when they came down."

"Mine too, I just wanted to be sure. But just because he mounts Judy doesn't mean he couldn't mount someone else."

Meatloaf was ahead of me. "Like Vicki. You think he goes over there to mount her?"

"Think about it. Judy goes away. Victor travels for work, too. Here's the key to Vicki's house. They play around at parties. He's got means, motive and opportunity."

"For murder?"

"No, for mounting," I said. "You know how he gets up before light-time and goes running sometimes? Maybe he runs to her house on the days when her mate isn't home."

"OK, so Robert mounts her. Is that bad?"

"Maybe it wasn't Bandit's male who made Vicki with-pup. What if it was Robert?"

He sat down. "I'm listening."

I thought my theory made the most sense. "Nobody wants to raise someone else's pup. Victor wouldn't want to raise Robert's pup."

Meatloaf cocked his head. "So he murders his own mate? How would Victor know whose pup it was? It could have been his own."

I hadn't figured that part out yet. "Maybe humans can smell their own pup."

"Nahh. She didn't even have a big stomach yet. She was at the park not that long ago with Nelly. You see a big stomach?"

"Nope."

Meatloaf got up and walked around the kitchen. "Where you goin' with this, dawg?"

"I think Victor is the murder-human. I think he killed his own mate."

He stopped and sniffed the key again. "Maybe. Or maybe it's Robert."

"Robert! How you figure?"

"Let's say Robert makes Vicki with-pup. She uses the test strips one day and finds out. Next she hides the strip from her mate so he doesn't know. Then she calls Robert and says what're you gonna do? Robert knows he's in trouble, he needs to hide it from Victor."

"So then Robert kills Vicki? Why would he do that?" I ask.

"That would take care of all his problems."

I knew this was wrong. "When could he have done it? We would have seen him leave the house that night."

"But he was up that night. Remember, he made us stop barking at the police and come inside the house."

Meatloaf was right, but that didn't mean he was a killer.

He went on. "Was he dressed in his clothes? Did he have shoes on? They don't wear those shoes to bed, you know."

"I don't know." I was very confused.

"When you went in Nelly's house, did you smell Robert's odor inside?"

"Yeah, sure. I smelled a lot of other neighbors, too."

"Where was Robert's smell the strongest?"

I thought about our visit that morning. It seemed like Robert's smell was mostly in the visitor bedroom.

"I don't remember."

"It could be Robert who did this. Taser, you gotta face it."

"You're wrong, partner. Don't say that."

"I know you love him. I know he was the one who pulled you out of that Pound. But if we're gonna look at this murder right, if we're gonna find out who did it, we got to consider everything."

"No! Robert couldn't murder his own kind."

Meatloaf looked at me hard. "In the right situation, anyone can kill."

After he said that, I had nothing more to say.

***

City of Phoenix Dog Pound

I see Zeus stop right in front of Major. He's all tense, like he's waiting for the command to kill. Major's back legs are flexed, waiting for the attack or the right moment. I back away as far as I think is safe, but I'm trembling like a little puppy. No one is barking, not even the crazy dogs. All you can hear is quiet panting, all you can smell is fear.

Zeus leaps.

Major sidesteps the attack and gets hold of Zeus' shoulder. He bites and shakes, trying to keep the Pitbull away from his neck. They battle on hind legs, claws digging at the concrete, searching for traction, advantage, escape. Their fierce growls are the only sound in the room. Major has long, powerful legs, and he pushes Zeus around and around, searching for a weak spot to shift his bite on the huge Pitbull.

There is no weak spot.

Zeus twists away and blood oozes from Major's attack. Now Zeus gets the big German Shepherd in his powerful grip and shakes him like a flimsy chew toy, over and over. They dance backwards but Major stumbles and goes down on his back. Zeus tightens his grasp on the soft throat as the Shepherd kicks helplessly under the weight of this furious mass. Major struggles in vain as Zeus shifts his awesome power to his jaws, clamping harder.

It's the end for Major and he knows it. His eyes catch mine, but all I can see is Cody's eyes staring helplessly. I'm still trembling as I smell my bladder empty, urine colors the concrete floor at our feet. I look down, ashamed at my show of weakness.

But it isn't my urine.

It isn't my bladder.

It's Major's.

When I see that happen, everything in my life changes, from the moment I was born until the moment I will die. I know if someone as fierce as Major is scared, that someone as scared as me can be fierce.

I don't think, I just act.

I leap on Zeus' body, aiming for the one weak spot Major never found. My teeth sink deep into Zeus' good eye, blinding his last vicious view of the world. He yelps and releases Major, then stumbles from the fight. Round and round he staggers, finally falling on his side.

But it's not enough for the ancient beast that takes over my body and fires my will to survive. I rip into Zeus' soft belly with years of anger and hate. I bite and tear and gnaw until his gore is all over him and all over the floor and all over me. I rip until he doesn't move anymore. I tear until I know Zeus will never kill another dog, never kill another friend.

Finally, I stand and turn around, blood dripping from my jowls. The circle of pound dogs stare quietly at me, then slowly back away. I look at Major. He's still on his side but his eyes are bright and clear. He lifts his head and nods at me--dog to dog, survivor to survivor.

FOURTEEN

It was not a noise we would normally hear on our street, that's why we started barking even before we got to the front window.

Thunk. Thunk. Thunk.

Meatloaf let the trespasser have it with his slow baritone bark, I was a little crazier, like I was about to attack and nothing could hold me back.

Thunk. Thunk. Thunk.

The trespasser didn't seem impressed. He had these poles or shovels or something, and he was digging a little hole in our front yard right by the street. He'd parked his pickup truck on the street next to where he was working. We stopped barking and watched, because the barking didn't seem to be doing much good. When he got the hole deep enough, he reached in the back of the truck, pulled out a post and stuck it in the hole. Then he hung a little sign on it.

Catcrap! I knew just what this was.

"What's he putting in there?" asked Meatloaf.

"A flip sign."

"That like a stop sign?"

"No, a flipper sign. They put those things in your front yard and pretty soon the flipper-humans come and your dog buddy and his humans move away. I don't know how many friends I've lost because of those signs."

"Flipper-humans?"

"The ones from that TV show"

"I knew it. That bonebreath Robert. I'm not sorry we took his steak, now."

The guy out front was still messing with the dirt from the hole. When he got it like he wanted, he put his poles and stuff in his truck and drove away, leaving us to worry about what was coming next.

103

I sat down and felt sorry for myself. Meatloaf went off in the kitchen to do somethin'. I heard him grunting and groaning.

"What're you doin' in there?" I asked.

Silence.

"Meatloaf."

Nothing.

"Meatloaf, what's happening?"

He called out from the kitchen. "I'm tryin' to get the cold-box open. I'm gonna take another steak."

I ran in to look. He had his mouth on the handle of the big silver cold-box.

"You're takin' another one?"

"For me this time. Since we're going to lockup, this is probably my last chance to get red meat."

He tugged a while longer, then he sat down with me.

"That thing is impossible," he said.

"They make 'em that way to keep dogs out. Otherwise there'd be no food left when they come home from work."

Meatloaf stared at the kitchen door out to the rear yard. "That's why humans put those round things on the doors."

"Well, you don't want strange dogs wanderin' in here anyway."

"Think how different our lives would be if we could turn those round things. I'm telling you, the man just wants to keep us down. I'm tired of this discrimination, it's specism."

"Meat. Come on. Don't exaggerate."

"You don't think they're prejudiced? How come they get to eat three times a day and we only get two meals?"

"You really think you need another meal?"

"That's not the point. We should be able to eat and leave when we want to."

I tried to be practical. "It's just as well. We'd be goin' out and gettin' run over by cars. Humans got this all stuff figured out, we should just go with it."

104

"The only place we're going to is to the Pound."

I wanted to cheer him up about that, but I was too upset myself. "We don't have much time left to catch this killer."

"Forget it. We got a better chance of learning to climb trees. If the police-humans can't find him, how can a pack of dogs?"

I jumped up and got face to face with him. "First thing, we got the nose for this. Our nose is better than any cop out there. Why do you think the police hire dogs for their department? And we got your brain and my brain and all the rest of the pack's brains. That's a lot of smells and a lot of smarts."

"All that and we still can't open a round door-thing."

"Meatloaf, you're not thinking clearly. You're just hungry. Robert will be home soon and he'll feed us."

"Maybe. Maybe not. We'll see after he finds out his steak is gone."

Meatloaf had a good point, but I didn't have time to worry about it, 'cause just then I heard the key in the front door. I figured Robert's friend must have dropped him off from work.

"Quick!"

We got out of the kitchen just in time. We were in the hall with our tails waggin' when Robert opened the front door.

Hi Guys.

We gave him a big goofy greeting, then we followed him in the kitchen to watch him open the letters. We got lucky with the steak, he didn't notice it missing. After the letter business he gave us second-meal, then he opened a beer and turned on the outside barbeque oven. After all that, Robert sat in front of the TV and we watched news-heads. There were a lot of angry faces and loud noises and grey smoke, just like every other night. It might have been a repeat, I'm not sure.

A little later he got up and went to the kitchen counter and stared down at it. Then he stared at the other counter and scratched his head. He looked over at us, but we put on the 'I-don't-know-catcrap' look. Finally Robert took another steak out of the cold box and put it in the glass cupboard with the bell.

Wow. Meatloaf had this trick down.

Robert watched the steak go around and around, and when the bell rang he took it out and cooked it in the outside oven. The day-light was low and it wasn't too warm outside, so we joined him on the patio. I noticed he liked a cold glass for his drink, just like we did. When the steak was done we lay in the kitchen to watch him eat. He talked to us while he ate, and we liked that a lot, except when he talked about baseballs.

Sometimes he lets us know how the diamond back baseballs were doing. It was always them and somebody else and then some numbers and somebody was the winner. Robert was happy when the diamond back baseballs won.

When the time came to go to the park I didn't want to go, I couldn't face the pack tonight. I didn't want them to hassle me. My dog life was a mess. I let someone steal our Jeep, my human was moving away and me and Meatloaf were goin' to the pound. How could it get any worse?

But I thought Simba might be there so I went along anyway. I still had hope.

It got dark early because these fast-moving' black clouds covered the sky. The air felt hot and thick, like you could take a bite out of it. On the way to the park, I got hit by some big rain drops.

Meatloaf trotted ahead for once. I saw Simba standing with Buffy by the big drainage pipe, they musta been lookin' for some of those irritating rabbits. Roxie and Gizmo and Winston were waiting at our usual spot.

I was glad I came when I saw my friend's panting faces.

"Hey dogs."

"Taser, get this." Roxie said. "I saw the police at Bandit's house today. I figure they were talking to his human about the murder. They were in there a long time, one guy in uniform and one guy in a suit."

"Probably a Detective Lieutenant," said Winston.

Winston had a way of appearing out of nowhere and immediately knowing everything.

Gizmo spoke up. "That means either they don't know who did it, or they think it's him."

"I don't think it's Bandit's human anymore," I said. "I think it's Victor. I think the guy killed his mate so he didn't have to raise some other human's pup."

"That's what lions do," said Winston. "When a new alpha-lion takes over a pack, he kills the pups of the others, so his pups live and the others don't." He spoke defensively at our stares. "I'm not daft, I saw it on the Animal Channel."

"We believe you, Winston."

"Speaking of Victor, isn't that him?"

We all turned to see a tall male walk up and greet our masters and neighbors talking at the Park sidewalk. Victor had hair on his face like some human breeds do. He wasn't smiling, but he acted friendly. There was a lot of hugging and handshaking, and then Victor talked to them about something we couldn't hear.

"Winston. Go see if you can catch what he's saying."

The feisty Bulldog scurried off on short legs. I had a lot of respect for the guy, I think he understood more words than any dog in the neighborhood. He was smart and older than most of us, so he'd learned a lot in his lifetime.

Meatloaf nudged my side. "Still think Victor's the killer?"

I looked at Victor closely, but I didn't know what a murder-human looked like. He seemed nice enough, even Robert shook his hand. Maybe we got off track with this mounting business. I guess it could have been an intruder or house robber. There were too-many suspects, it made my brain hurt sorting them out.

I spoke my thoughts to the pack. "OK, so maybe it wasn't Victor. Wasn't a camera stolen from their house? He wouldn't steal his own camera, would he?"

"That's right," said Gizmo. "And the rear window was broken. He wouldn't need to break in his own house, either."

"Bandit's human would," I offered.

Then Meatloaf stuck his paw in his mouth.

"Robert wouldn't need to, he has a key to Nelly's house."

I wished Meatloaf hadn't said that, but it was too late. Simba and Buffy showed up just in time to hear him tell the group.

"Your male has a key to Nelly's house?" Buffy asked. "What's that about?"

I tried to mumble my way out of it. "Uhmm. He waters their bushes when they go on vacation."

She gave me a funny look, but I think she bought it.

Simba stood close to me. It seemed my friends still liked me, even if I had messed up guarding our Jeep. Then she asked me about the flipper-sign.

"Taser, are your humans selling their house?"

"That's what it looks like. Judy doesn't like the neighborhood anymore. She doesn't want to live with murders down the street."

Meatloaf spoke up. "That's why we gotta find out who did it. So they won't move away."

"Yeah," said Roxie.

"That's right," said Gizmo.

Buffy had her own opinion. "I hope my humans decide to move. If the murder-humans don't kill you, the heat surely will. This beastly weather isn't fit for a dog."

Comments like that always made me crazy. "This is a shock to you? That it's hot in the desert? How can you can move to a desert and then complain 'cause it's hot?"

"I wasn't bred for this environment," she sniffed. "I'm not your kind."

"What were you bred for?" Meatloaf nosed her puffy coat. "Mopping the toilet?"

Simba came to her friend's defense. "Meatloaf, be nice. She's a Bichon, she can't help how her coat looks, her humans fluff it up."

Just then Winston ran up, panting.

"OK. If I heard right, Vicki's funeral is Friday, early in the light-time."

"What's a funeral?" asked Meatloaf.

Roxie knew all about it. "It's like a party, but nobody has any fun. They wear black clothes and sit on chairs and cry. Sometimes they get up and sniff the dead person. Then they bury him and everyone goes to lunch."

Winston picked up where he left off. "She's right about that. But after Vicki's funeral, everyone's coming over to Victor's house. He invited the whole blinkin' neighborhood over. Probably not us dogs, though."

"You see." Meatloaf stamped his paw. "That's what I'm talking about. Specism."

Gizmo looked confused. "So it's afterward they're having the party?"

"No, no," said Simba. "Not a party. It's just friends getting together to talk more. My human had people over when her mother died."

"Seems creepy to me," Gizmo said. "A human died at that house."

I thought about it. "It's all cleaned up inside. No human could smell anything."

"Maybe they want to start the healing process," said Meatloaf. "They probably need to exorcise any demons in their dwelling."

"All right," I said. "So this funeral party is Friday."

"Right. Whenever Friday is," said Roxie.

"I get these human names mixed up myself. I know day is what they call light-time, but these other names confuse me. Friday, Saturday, Sunday."

"Sunday was yesterday," said Simba.

"What's today?"

"Moon day," said Meatloaf.

109

"You clear on that?" asked Winston.

Meatloaf nodded. "Yep. Moon is what the humans call the nightlight. They name days after planets in the sky. Moon day. Sun day. Saturn day."

Winston looked skeptical. "That's daft. What about the others? What about Fry day, Thirst day, Weds day?"

"And Tunes day," said Simba.

Everyone looked at Meatloaf.

He seemed to know all about it.

"Those are the planets they haven't discovered yet. They're named after the humans working on it now.

"No offense, Meatloaf, but maybe we should get a second opinion on that," said Winston.

"We could TeeVee it. Maybe the Discovery Channel has something," offered Gizmo.

"What about Days of Our Lives?" said Buffy. "It's on every morning."

"No Buffy, I think that's something different. Nelly would know, she was such a smart dog." Simba hung her head. "I really miss her."

It'd been a while since I thought about her. "Where's Nelly living? If we could talk to her, we could solve this whole mess. She's an eyewitness, she knows who did this murder."

The pack nodded muzzles, but no one knew where she was staying. All we'd heard was she was staying with friends.

"Maybe she'll come to the house after the funeral," Simba said.

I doubted it.

I didn't think we'd ever see Nelly again.

***

Dominga was late.

I wondered what her life was like, hiding during the day, trying to stay cool, roaming at night hunting food and water. She seemed to

110

hate humans, maybe that's why her kind never stayed with them. Or maybe she hated them for what they did to coyotes.

I knew not all humans were good. I'd had a bad one once myself, but there's not much else a dog can do. We have to stay with them. We gotta eat. We can't just go out in the desert and kill our own dinner. Food first. We'll take love after that, if we can get it.

It was sprinkling rain now and then, but it wasn't much cooler, even with the wind. Lightning flashed crazily down in the Phoenix Valley and it smelled like it was raining someplace close by. The brewing storm reminded me of that night Nelly howled for help, the night my life took a bad turn.

I was so confused about the murder that I didn't know what to think, except it seemed us dogs would never find who did it. There were too many clues, too many possible murder-humans. I felt like I'd failed in my investigation, so I thought I'd appeal to Dominga one more time.

After Robert went to bed, me and Meatloaf dug up the steak, then he went inside to sleep. I had the steak sitting on my side of the fence so Dominga could smell it but not take it. I hated to be that way, but maybe food for information was the way with her.

All of a sudden she appeared out of nowhere, it gave me a start.

"Oh," I said. It just came out.

She sniffed close to the fence. "What is this you bring?"

"It's meat. For you." But I didn't move to give it to her.

She sat down. "You want me to beg. You want me to be like your kind, begging for food." Not a question, a fact.

"No. I don't want you to beg. I hoped we could trade food for information. I need to know if you saw anyone out in the desert that night, and if they went over the fence to the house."

She stood and stared at me. "Then you want me to do worse than beg. You want me to betray another outlaw."

"No Dominga. You're not an outlaw. That's the name some would call you, but it's not what I believe."

"My family will go hungry first."

111

"I need your help to find this human killer," I said.

"So. Now you come to my kind for help. Why don't go to your humans? You go to them for food. You go to them for your lair. You go to them for protection. But now you come to your brothers and sisters?"

"We do use humans, it's true. I need them to survive. It was my father's way and all the fathers before him. It's not my choice."

"You grow weak in their house."

"Please, I'm begging you."

She sniffed. "I will never help your humans."

"Why? What did humans do to you?"

Dominga looked up at the nightlight peaking over the mountain. "The two small-ones I have now, they are not my first. My last three died from no food, it was the time of no water, no prey. But before that time, rains fell strong, prey filled the land. I had four small-ones, they were my first born. They grew big and strong until they were ready to go out on their own."

She hung her head now, she wouldn't look at me.

"I went out to hunt and killed a fat rabbit for them, but when I came close to our lair, there was a man with a long-stick making loud noise, very-loud noise. Four times I heard this sound. I could only hide and watch. When he left and I came to my lair, all my small ones were dead. With them died all my hope."

Her fiery-yellow eyes narrowed. "That is when I met evil itself."

Just when I thought I couldn't feel any worse. "I'm sorry, Dominga. I understand." I bit the steak and put it up and through the fence. "You need to stay strong. But this much is true: Just like your kind, not all humans are bad. When you hurt this murder-human, you hurt evil."

I backed away so she could take it. My troubles seemed so minor now, I felt I could manage things on my own. I turned to go.

"Wait," she said.

I turned back. She hadn't moved or touched the meat.

"I can tell you this. The night of the howling dog, a man came out of the desert. I was very close to him, but he did not see me. He went straight to the house and climbed over the fence."

I was excited, this meant it wasn't my Robert. "An intruder, then. I knew it."

"What is this, intruder? What does that mean?"

"A stranger. A bad man from the big city who comes to steal or kill."

I saw her hesitate.

"You have more?" I asked. "Please, what is it?"

"This man. He came from the desert that night, this is true. But he lives in one of your many houses. He is one of your close humans, I know his smell."

"No!" I ran right up to the metal fence. "Who? Who is it?"

"I'm sorry, Taser. I will say no more. I hope this helps you."

She grabbed the steak and ran off into the darkness.

"Dominga! Who is it!"

I yelled after her again.

The only thing that answered was the wind.

FIFTEEN

Robert was up before the light.

He started with that loud, annoying machine they use, the one they push all over the floor. We got up and moved out of the way, but pretty soon he followed us and we had to move again. It does somethin' to the carpet that they like, but I can't see any difference. Then he rubbed the kitchen counters and put his papers and stuff into drawers. When he was done in there, he wiped all the windows with a cloth, then he got that stick with a rag on the end. He pushed that all over the tile floor.

Me and Meatloaf were a little upset, 'cause this was messin' up our morning routine. Normally, after we get first meal and Robert goes to work, we go outside to chase away any birds, lizards or cats that may have taken over the back yard. Then we come in, drink a little water and watch our favorite TV shows. Most times we'd sleep. Today he was cramping our style.

"Isn't this a work day for him?" Meatloaf asked.

"I know, I don't get it."

"Must be a party tonight."

Then Robert went out in the yard and picked up our poop and chew toys. I thought maybe he wasn't goin' to work at all until he went upstairs and changed into his shiny-shoe clothes. Pretty soon somebody honked their car horn out front and Robert went out. As he left, he made a point to tell us to be good dogs.

"Why'd he say that?" I asked Meatloaf.

"Something's up. He wouldn't be having a party tonight without Judy, unless she's coming home today."

"Maybe it's her birth day. They make a fuss about birth days."

"I don't think so, it's too early for her to be home. She usually stays away longer."

I went to the front window and looked out to check the yard. All I could see was one of those annoying rabbits out front eating our plants. If I could just work those round door-things, I'd show 'em who the alpha animal was at this house. But then I saw the flipper sign in the yard, and I knew what was up.

"Meatloaf. He's got flip-humans comin' today. He's got some people comin' to look at the house, that's why he cleaned it up."

"Well, catcrap."

"One of 'em will stick us in the hot garage while they look at our house. We're gonna have flip-humans in here, droolin' like dogs at meal time over our stuff."

"That really burns me up, dawg. What if somebody buys the place? We could be out of here next-day. We may never see our pack friends again."

I could hardly believe Robert would do something like this to us. After all the work we're doin' to find the murder-human for him and Judy.

"We'll know for sure if somebody comes by early and bakes cookies," I said.

"Why? They think we'll sell out for a little food? They think they can buy us off with cookies?" Meatloaf thought a minute. "Wait, what kind of cookies?"

"Probably chocolate chip. They may give us one, but they're only baking them for the smell. It's a Flipper trick, they do it all the time on that show. They bake some cookies so the house smells like a nice place to live." It was hard to believe humans were that dumb. On the other hand, I'd seen a lot of their television shows.

"So if it smells nice in here, they might buy it. Right?" he asked.

"Right."

"But if it smells bad…"

"Meatloaf, you're a genius. Where should we do it?"

He trotted in the living room. "I've found if you have to pee inside, it's best to do it under the table or behind the couch. You don't get caught because it dries before they find it. It does smell, though."

I shook my muzzle. "Human noses aren't sensitive enough to pee. Not the males, anyway. I think we have to drop the big one, nobody likes that smell."

Meatloaf looked surprised. "Dawg, that's a serious violation. You sure?"

"Bigger the better. Put it behind the couch so they can't find it and clean up."

"I don't think I can go, how about you?"

"I went this morning." I tried to figure out what we could do, but I wasn't sure how much time we had. "Can't you eat some seed pods?"

"Takes too long. I'll go in the pantry and check the shelves."

I was a little nervous 'cause we were into major dog-felony territory. On the other hand, how much worse could it get? We needed a little more time to figure this murder out, I was gettin' desperate.

I yelled at him. "Find anything?"

"Nothing on the bottom shelf."

Robert usually leaves the pantry door open because we been so good for so long. He trusted us.

"What about oatmeal?" Meatloaf called out.

"Not quick enough. Keep lookin'." I thought someone could show up any time, so we couldn't chance waiting.

Then Meatloaf trotted around the corner with a bag in his mouth. He dropped it at my feet. "This smells like dried fruit," he said.

I sniffed it. "Yeah. Prunes, I think. Or maybe apricots, I always get those two mixed up. You want me to help?"

"Nah, no sense both of us getting sick."

He held the bag with his front paws and tore it open with his teeth, and then he ate one.

"Dawg, these are great."

116

"Go for it."

He kept eatin' until the bag was gone. It didn't take long.

"Feel anything yet?" I asked.

Meatloaf burped. "Not yet. I'll drink some water."

I put the bag in the little recycle bucket while he went over to the water dish and drank half the bowl.

"Nothing yet," he said.

While we were waiting I told Meatloaf about my talk with Dominga last night. He thought it was both good news and bad news. We knew it was someone in our neighborhood, but we just couldn't put our paw on the guy yet. At least we were makin' progress.

"Why won't she tell you who it is?" he asked.

"She says she hates humans and she doesn't want to help them."

"She's mad—"

Suddenly Meatloaf hunched over.

"Oh-oh."

He hurried to the living room and crouched behind the couch. He was there for a while, it sounded messy if not promising. Finally he came back in the kitchen, walkin' sideways and a little shaky.

"Wow. I wouldn't want to clean that up," Meatloaf said. He looked happy and energetic. "I feel great, though. You should've had some of that fruit."

Just then, I smelled the doggie surprise invade this side of the house. It was bad.

"Maybe we overdid it," I said.

Meatloaf looked up at the ceiling. "Hope the fire alarm doesn't go off."

"Outside, quick." My eyes watered so bad I didn't think I could find the dog door. But we made it out and went to the patio shaded by the big Mesquite. We stretched out and waited for somebody to visit our house.

117

I got a little warm after a while, but I didn't worry about it. I knew the lawn sprinklers would be coming on soon, and we could always lie on the wet grass to cool off, just liked I'd seen the rabbits do.

I thought of Nelly's swimming pool sitting there unused and wished we had one to swim in. I loved to swim, but I don't think I ever saw my partner get in the water.

"Hey Meat, wouldn't it be nice to have our own swimming pool? I could use a swim about now."

"Ehh."

"You're not hot?"

"I'm not much for swimming."

"What're you talkin' about, Labs are natural swimmers, we even have webbed feet."

"I'm not happy about that."

"Meatloaf, you're a Lab from Labrador. We're bred for swimming in the cold Atlantic ocean. "

"I'd swim in the ocean, that's cool. I just don't like swimming pools. They put all that chlorine in there. It's bad for the environment."

"Your drinking water has chlorine in it," I said.

"Not as much. The big problem with drinking water is fluoride. That's why I drink out of the big white water dish when I can. They don't put fluoride in the bathroom water. It's too valuable."

I paused to scratch my ribs, wondering where Meatloaf learned this stuff. "What's your problem with fluoride?"

"It melts your bones. After years of drinking fluoride water, your teeth and your bones get soft. Even dog bones melt."

"Why would they give you somethin' that melts your bones? That doesn't make any sense."

"It's a conspiracy. The doctors and the dentists and the vets worked together to make us drink fluoride. They're all in it together with the drugging companies."

"Who told you all this?"

"My human in Fresno. He read it in the computer. They've been doing it for years and years and now it's finally paying off for them."

"These are the same vet-humans that help us when we're sick."

"Yeah, for money."

"That doesn't affect us dogs. They need money for their work."

"That's my point. Think of the money they'll make when we all get soft bones. It's big business, you've seen those TV ads."

I didn't know what he was talking about. "What ads?"

"They're on every station. Males get soft first, usually when they get a little older. They try to mount some female and wham, nothing happens. You're still young, but I know all about this, trust me. It's like pushing on a leash. Humans take these little purple pills for it."

Now I remembered seeing those ads. "Those drugging companies must be rich."

"My Fresno human knew all that secret stuff, like who killed Kennedy, all those other things they don't want us to know."

I held up a paw to silence Meatloaf. "Listen."

A car pulled slowly up in front of our house and stopped with the motor running. Then I heard doors opening and closing, so I thought this might be it. We ran to the gate and looked out, but we didn't bark.

It was one male-human and two females getting out of a new car. They were dressed in shiny-shoe clothes, but two of them looked like mates from another country. Their clothes were too dark for the hot time. They looked uncomfortable, like some dogs do when they have too-much hair for our Phoenix desert. Not that I should talk, I was wearin' black myself, but hey, I think it looks good on me.

I wondered why humans didn't pant when they were hot. It had to be those little lips again, they were just better than ours.

One of the female humans must've been the alpha flipper, 'cause she was doin' all the talking. She pointed at our house and she pointed at the park, and she pointed at the neighbor's houses. Then they walked up the driveway toward the front door.

"Meat. Run in and listen to what they say."

119

Meatloaf went in the dog door while I waited outside in the day-light. I thought about going inside and attacking them like a rabid dog, but I thought the poop trick would work better. I was right. It seemed like the humans came out right away, in less time than it took to eat a bowl of dog food. Pretty soon Meatloaf was back.

"You should have seen it," he said. "The females put their hand on their nose and whined like puppies. It's still pretty bad in there."

"Did they see you?"

"Nah. I hid around the corner. I'm not sure what they said, but I don't think they want to live here anymore."

I heard the car doors slam and the humans drive away.

"Nice work, Meatloaf."

"A pleasure."

SIXTEEN

I was nervous when I heard Robert's key in the door, but I was ready to take my punishment.

Meatloaf and I sat side by side in the hallway. Robert came in the front door and dropped his briefcase on the floor.

Meatloaf! Taser! What is that?

He looked around for the source of the smell.

We hung our head and tried to look pathetic. I figured we couldn't get in too-much trouble since he wouldn't know for sure which dog pooped in the house. Hanging your head is very important, though. You have to show you're sorry before you get forgiveness.

Robert searched the living room floor until he found the mess behind the couch. I was glad it was weird colors, 'cause they think you can't hold it when it's like that. So I didn't expect a lot of yellin', but I certainly didn't expect what happened next. Robert came over to us, got down on the floor and hugged us both around the neck.

Who wants a bone?

I couldn't believe it. He went in the pantry and gave us each a big milk bone before we even got our normal second meal. While we ate our treat in the kitchen, Robert got some cleaning stuff and a bucket and cleaned up Meatloaf's mess in the living room. We stayed out of there. I looked at Meatloaf and shrugged, he shrugged back. We couldn't figure it out.

"What's up with him?"

"Beats me," I said.

"Musta had a great day at work."

I didn't think so. It seemed like he knew about the smell before he came in the house, he didn't make enough fuss when he walked in. Maybe the flipper-human told him the bad news before he came home.

When he was done, Robert opened all the windows and turned on the fans. It took a little while but the smell mostly went away.

Then we got our second-meal. We didn't want to push our luck, so we stayed on good behavior while he made some spaghetti for his dinner. We didn't beg for a taste of his dinner like we usually do. If he makes spaghetti with meatballs, there's always a spare meatball for us. But tonight he put some kinda stinky fish in the pan, which seemed like a waste of good sauce to me.

Robert seemed to be in a good mood, he talked a lot to us as he ate. Sometimes I think he gets lonely when Judy isn't here, but it's hard for me to figure out human mates. It's never like it seems. I didn't have a mate, but I know I would be lonely without a buddy like Meatloaf. So we tried to be good company for Robert. We listened closely, even when he talked about baseball numbers and humans we didn't know.

***

Pretty soon it was time for our walk to the park. I was always ready for the park, but I wasn't ready for the news I got when I met the pack. They were excited about something new. Very excited.

Roxie spoke first. "You guys hear? The police got him!"

"What are you talkin' about?"

"The killer." Simba seemed very happy. "They solved the case. The Scottsdale Police are charging him with Vicki's murder."

I was confused. "They're charging Bandit's male?"

"No, the robber, the one they call the Boulder Bandit. The one who's been hitting all the expensive houses up here for a year."

Winston jumped in. "He gets in the back yard and breaks a window with a rock from the victim's yard. He hits houses where people are away or on vacation."

"Wait, why'd they think this guy murdered her?"

122

"Same M.O." said Winston. "Vicki's rear window was broken with a big rock. The police think Vicki surprised him. He must have thought everyone was gone, but it was just Victor out of town. You ever watch the local news channel?"

This was coming at me too fast, I could hardly believe it. "So, this robber, he's been doing this for a year? And he lives right here in our neighborhood?"

"No, no," said Gizmo. "He lives in Tucson. He comes up once a month to do a robbery, and then he'd lay low until next month."

I wasn't buying this pinch. "No way. It couldn't be the Boulder Bandit."

"Why not?" Gizmo asked. "You said it could be an intruder."

I hesitated. "He's not from our neighborhood."

"Big deal."

I was about to say something when Remi and Bandit arrived.

Simba nudged Winston. "Tell them."

Winston nodded. "They caught the murder-human. It was some blagger from Tucson who busts houses here in Scottsdale. The cops got him now."

"Thank Heavens," said Remi.

"Fine," said Bandit. "We can move on from this stupid investigation. I told you these matters were better left to the police."

"Let the professionals handle it," Remi agreed.

"Wait," I said. "It can't be this guy. It's someone from this neighborhood, I know for sure."

"Oh, please," said Remi.

Roxie objected, too. "Taser, what's your problem? You ought to be happy, maybe now your humans won't sell your house."

"How can you know for sure it ain't him?" asked Gizmo.

The whole pack turned and looked at me. I didn't know what to say.

Unfortunately, Meatloaf did. "Taser talked to an eyewitness. She saw the whole thing."

"Meatloaf—" I tried to stop him but it was too late. The pack was all over me now.

"She?" asked Simba.

"Eyewitness?" asked Winston.

Gizmo cocked his head. "What's up with that?"

I couldn't say anything. I couldn't tell them I'd been talking to Dominga, no one would understand.

Bandit seemed happy about my discomfort. "What's the matter, Taser, cat got your tongue?"

He had a twinkle in his eye that put me on guard.

"Please, we're dying to know. Tell us more," he said.

I didn't say anything, so Bandit kept talkin' to the pack.

"There's a good reason Taser won't tell you who this eyewitness is. Right, Taser?" He looked at me with a smirk.

I was startin' to pant under the pressure.

"I'd like to let the pack in on something," Bandit said. "Where's Buffy?"

Simba pointed. "She's out in the park looking for rabbits."

We looked. She was out smelling the grass by the drainage pipe.

"I'll tell her later." Bandit waited for everyone's attention, then he continued. "We've all been talking about neighborhood security. I'm as concerned as anymutt, and I do my part, just like you. But there's something going on here you should be aware of."

Meatloaf gave me a funny look.

"I live a few houses down from Taser and Meatloaf. And like all of you, I watch the neighborhood. I'm here to tell you something terrible has been going on right under our noses." He pointed his paw at me. "For many days, now, Taser has been attracting coyotes to our neighborhood by feeding them through his fence."

Simba looked at me, horrified. "Taser, is that true?"

I froze like I'd been caught with my head deep in the dog-food bag.

Bandit went on. "I've been watching through my back fence, across the desert. After the neighborhood is asleep, coyotes come to Taser's

124

house for the food he puts out. He's teaching them they have nothing to fear from us dogs!"

"No!"

"Taser, tell us he's lying."

"Is that your eyewitness, a coyote? How dare you!"

I didn't know what to say. "Look, it's a female and…"

"You're feeding a female coyote?" Simba raised her voice. 'What's she doing for you in return?"

Even Gizmo was shocked. "Meatloaf, is this true? What's your partner been up to?"

Meatloaf looked defensive. "He's just helping our brothers in their time of need."

"Brothers?" Remi seemed amused by that. "These are vicious killers you're helping. Carnivores. Scavengers. Low-life garbage eaters."

"What's wrong with garbage?" Meatloaf asked.

I tried to explain myself. "These animals want to live, just like we do. They were here in the desert before we came and destroyed their way of life. They're no different than us."

"How could you?" Simba glared at me.

I couldn't argue with her, she was too angry. I stood there, helpless, as she ran out in the park to tell Buffy.

Bandit got right in my face. "So, big dog, who's the buttsniffer now?"

"I—." There was nothing I could say that would make it right.

He and Remi walked away, following Simba to Buffy.

I turned to my remaining friends. "I'm sorry I didn't tell you guys before, I didn't think you'd understand. But she did see a human from our neighborhood go over Vicki's fence."

"How do you know she's telling the truth?" asked Gizmo. "She could say anything to get food from you."

I thought a moment about the steak I gave her.

Even Winston looked upset with me. "They're filthy, lying creatures. They'd just as soon slit your throat as look at you."

125

"Winston, she's not like that at all. She's a mother with pups."

"Now we're gonna have even more coyotes around here?" Roxie asked. "You should have cleared it with us, Taser."

That burned me a little. "So I have to get permission from you to help a starving animal? Who are you to tell me I can't help?"

Meatloaf stepped in the middle. "Hey, cool it, dogs. Can't we all just get along?"

We stood in silence, panting from the heat or the argument. I thought it was time for me and Meatloaf to go.

I started to say so, but I was cut off by a chilling scream from the far side of the park.

Simba!

I jerked my head around where I'd seen her last. Bandit and Remi were running away from that spot, coming back toward us. Simba stood alone, barking furiously at a flash of grey and white.

The white was Buffy.

The grey was a full-size coyote.

I burst out of the pack, running as fast as I could.

A big male had Buffy clamped in his mouth as he ran to the drainage pipe. He ducked down and ran inside. I was many dog-lengths behind but I didn't give up. I chased him through the long pipe, finally coming out in the open desert at the other end.

I couldn't see him anywhere.

I strained to see in the weak light, looking high and low and straight ahead to the mountains.

The coyote had vanished.

I put my nose down and ran, his scent was everywhere, he must've come to this area every day for rabbits. I ran up one trail and down the other, franticly searching the bushes and washes for the big male. His smell filled the air and soaked the rock-strewn desert, but I couldn't find him. I couldn't find Buffy either, just tufts of her hair and drops of her blood.

126

Finally, I turned around and looked across to the park to my sheltered life on the civilized side of the fence.

Robert called my name. Taserrrrr!

The pack barked madly. Woof woof! Bow wow! Arf arf! Yip yip yip!

I heard my friend's calls.

I smelled Buffy's blood.

But all I could see—in the failing light—was my little world crumbling down on the desert floor.

SEVENTEEN

Finally, the rain came.

The storm started like any other hot-time blow. The wind was light at first, but it built stronger, ripping branches from our Mesquite trees and sending them crashing down in the back yard. Flying paper and loose trash chased each other around the yard. Just before the downpour, thick dust filled the air, making it hard to breathe or see. But still I didn't go in the house with Meatloaf, even when he begged. I needed to be miserable.

I huddled deep in my dog house on the patio, trying to stay dry as rain blew under the patio roof, soaking the floor outside my little house. Lightning flashed so close I thought it might hit our trees. I could see the desert light-up with each blinding strike. I heard Harley next door, barking at the wind and the rain, even from the safety of his house. He sounded scared.

Then everything went black. The storm knocked out the electricity to our neighborhood, making the lightning seem even closer and brighter in the darkness. More neighborhood dogs started barking in their homes, dogs that use to be my friends.

It didn't matter. I'd been alone before.

I was mad at myself for being wrong about the coyotes. I should have known they wouldn't care about the difference between a steak and a rabbit, a large cat or a small dog. They were all food to a coyote. Dominga said they would eat humans if they could. It was just that humans were bigger and more dangerous than a harmless little Bichon Frise.

I was so sorry she died.

I hoped it wasn't my fault.

But I feared it was.

I didn't know if Dominga came to the fence tonight looking for food and I didn't care. I wasn't going to help her kind any more. Not that it mattered. It was too late for it to make a difference.

Simba was so mad at me she barked and nipped me as she went by, and it wasn't a love bite. Bandit had plenty to say about me to the pack, also. They were all mad at me—Winston, Roxie, even Gizmo. The only friend I had left was Meatloaf.

So I was alone tonight, but that's how I wanted it, alone with my pain and my guilt and my stupid clues to the murder. I put my back against the leather briefcase and looked out at the frantic rain. It was cooler now, almost cold in the wet air.

It seemed like everyone thought the Boulder Bandit was our human. Everyone except me. I didn't think so, even if the police did. These humans don't know everything. Look at Robert, he wants to get rid of us and move to an apartment just to make Judy happy.

Harley barked even more. Sometimes I think he's a little loony, probably whacked from being in the house all the time. He must have thought there was something threatening outside. I lifted my head unconsciously and looked out into the night. When lightening flashed again, something seemed wrong. Something seemed very wrong, but I didn't know what it was.

Harley was still barking. He was nervous or scared, it wasn't an absent-minded bark—it was a warning.

I rose to my feet and stared at the night, waiting. It seemed like a long time passed.

Lightning struck and this time my head jerked back in shock. Not from the flash, but from what it revealed far out in the desert.

It was a man.

He was hunched over and peering straight into our back yard.

I trembled with the anticipation of a fight, but I resisted my first urge to bark. I needed to see who this was before I scared him away. When

129

the lightning struck again he was even closer. I strained to pick out something familiar about him. I tested the air with my nose, but I couldn't pick up a scent in the raging storm.

I stepped out of my dog house and walked out in the rain, advancing slowly toward the menace. Whoever this was, he wasn't getting over my fence. Finally I stood next to the metal bars, he should be very close by. Now I'd find out who he was.

The lightning flashed again.

No!

He was gone.

Bow wow wow wow wow!

I couldn't wait any longer. I had to tell him I was here to defend my home.

Bow wow wow wow!

Immediately Meatloaf was at my side, barking savagely.

Woof Woof Woof Woof!

"What is it, Taser?"

"Out there." I stared at the desert. Lightning flared, illuminating the wet brush and scraggly trees behind our house. It was no use, the man had vanished. Maybe he had seen me. Maybe I was wrong. We stood a long time in the rain but I never saw him again.

"I'm sorry Meatloaf, I thought I saw something."

"What'd you see? Snake? Bobcat?"

"A human. A big male."

"A male? What?"

"I might be wrong, but I swear I saw a human out there watching our house, a big guy. He was crouched over, lookin' in our back yard like he was watchin' us."

"Poochpoop!"

"Let's get out of this storm."

We moved under the patio roof and shook ourselves off, then stood close to the house to get out of the wind-blown rain.

"It was a big guy. Or a big bush. I'm not sure, now."

"Don't doubt yourself, Taser. I'm sure you saw somebody, there's been to much strange stuff happening lately."

I shook more water from my coat. "Yeah. You're probably right."

But I wasn't sure.

***

I spent the rest of the night in the dog house. Every once in a while I'd get up and check our yard, but all was calm. I was a happy dog when the rain finally quit. I got sleep when I could, but I woke up tired and sore from the hard doghouse floor.

The morning was quiet and predictable.

After Robert left for work, Meatloaf and I did our usual routine, but I was in no mood to watch television when he was ready to nap. I needed to get out and nose around, to see what was out there. It seemed like time was runnin' out and we may never solve this crime.

I decided right there that it was gonna be up to me. If no one else cared, fine, I'd just go out on my own.

I let Meatloaf sleep while I went out to our sideyard gate and looked up and down the street. I didn't see anyone, so I decided to bust out and cruise the neighborhood. I took a run at the gate and scratched my way up to flip the latch. This time I got it on the second try.

The gate popped open and I went out.

It felt like the good old days on the Westside, me trottin' down the sidewalk, checkin' out the sights. I cruised right by Roxie's house, then Bandit's. Not a peep from them. They musta been inside sleepin' the day away like Meatloaf. They'd thank me when I solved this murder.

I headed out toward the park, but stopped at a corner when I realized Spike lived somewhere on this street. I didn't know which house, but I figured the old Doberman wouldn't be hard to find. I thought I'd turn up the heat and ask him some direct questions.

I trotted down his street, nose up and working hard. A pickup truck cruised by with some worker guys wearin' hats in front, they were the first people I'd seen. They were cool, they didn't look twice at me.

131

They had a lot of long tree branches in the back, so I figured they were probably storm cleanup guys. There were still a lot of leaves and trash on the streets from the big blow last night. There was a lot of water around, too. I panted as I jogged, the rain left the air hot and thick.

I'd never been down this street by myself, I was always on a leash with Robert, so everything looked different, everything but the houses. They all looked the same to me, all light grey with tile roofs. Some had those top-story rooms, some didn't. I wasn't sure how humans found their way home, seein' as how they can't hardly smell at all. Maybe that's why all the yards looked different.

I paused to sniff some trash on the curb that somebody left out for the big truck, but nothin' seemed worth stoppin' for. Besides, I was on official business and neither cats nor rabbits or quail were gonna get me sidetracked. Time was short and some human could turn me in at any time. Humans around here get nervous when they see a dog walkin' alone. They think we're rabid or we're gonna bite their spoiled little pup-humans.

So I kept movin'.

I passed by about six or seven houses before I caught a hint of garlic and wet dog. I thought this could be it. I went over the grass yard right up to the gate. Yeah, it smelled like Spike, near as my nose could remember. I scratched on the gate and waited. Nothin'. I tried again. Finally I barked quietly.

Woof.

I see the dog door swing up and a pointy black and brown muzzle stick out, then a whole head appears. Spike looks right at me with sleepy eyes.

I bark again, a friendly greeting, nothin' rude.

Woof.

He steps slowly out the door and comes up, and we sniff noses through the wood slats. He doesn't seem too concerned about me trespassin' on his yard. He must've remembered me.

"You're one of that pack from the park," he says.

132

"Taser."

"That's right, and your buddy's Meatball."

"Meatloaf," I told him.

"Meatball, Meatloaf, what's the difference?"

"No pasta. You oughta know that, you're big on Italian food, aren't you?"

He ignored the crack and asked me something else.

"Whacha up to?"

"Nothin'. I got out of the yard, so I thought I'd cruise the neighborhood."

He shot me a skeptical look. "Cruise the neighborhood. And ya just happen to end up over here."

"Right. Just to talk."

"Too bad. I'm not much for talkin."

"Is it the talk or the subject?" I asked

Spike hesitated. "Depends."

"I thought we could discuss the murder at Nelly's place."

He looked to either side of him. "Why? I know from nothin'. Even if I did, you'd be da last to know."

"You must know somethin' that can help us dogs. Anything."

"Why? Dis is your problem, not mine."

I wasn't having much luck with this mutt. "You say you don't know nothin', but you're afraid to talk about it. If you're not guilty of somethin', what're you afraid of?"

That set him off. He bristled and he stuck his face right up to the fence.

"Lemme ask you a question, Blackie. Who made you a mountin' police dog?"

It was a fair question. But I was here for answers. "Look. Let's cut the catcrap. I know you're not from Cottonwood. I know you're not who you pretend to be."

Spike backed up. "Nice a ya to come by. I gotta go in now, it's time for my bath."

He started toward to his dog door, so I tried my last trick. "I know about the witness protection program."

Spike froze in his tracks, then turned around and came back to the fence and stared at me.

"What kinda mutt are you? You wit da Feds? Undercoverdog? Or just a nosey Lassie?"

"I'm the neighborhood snoop. But I'm not the neighborhood gossip, your secret's safe with me."

He looked at me hard. "It better be."

"Tell me this much. Was your human out last night?"

He looked up and down the street, like he was thinking before he answered. "Look. Blackie. You're barkin' up the wrong tree. Used to be, my master was out all night, most all da time. Now, he's an old guy, like me. He falls asleep snorin' on the couch right after dinner. He's as harmless as a kitten wit no claws."

I believed him, I never thought there was anything to Winston's theory. "Spike, I'm just lookin' for help. Whatever your human might've done in the past, he's made up for it. The law obviously thinks he's redeemed himself."

"So wadda you want from me?"

"Information. Whatever I can use to help me solve this crime. I'm not sayin' you know anything first-hand about this stuff, I'm just speakin' hypothetically."

He seemed interested. "Yeah, OK, I'll bite."

"This female human who was murdered, her throat was cut."

"Damn. Harlem Sunset. Tough way to go."

"I imagine there would be a lot of blood."

"Dis is true."

"And this blood would be all over the room, all over the murderer."

"Only if da guy was an amateur. A pro wouldn't get a drop on him, just his hands. And he'd be wearin' gloves."

That was interesting. "Let's say this guy's an amateur, he'd have to clean up before he left the house. He couldn't be caught with blood on his clothes, walkin' down the street."

Spike was gettin' into it. "Or if he's drivin', he wouldn't wanna be pulled over by da cops wit blood on him."

"And he'd have to get rid of the murder weapon, or destroy it."

"Was it a knife or a straight razor?"

"Knife. That's what the police said."

"Yeah, he'd wanna ditch the shiv. Unless…"

His voice trailed off.

"What? What're you thinkin'? "

Spike looked over his shoulder. "Hypo-thetically speakin', of course. Say the perp breaks into dis human's house. He gonna off the female. All he's gotta do is head to the silverware drawer for a sharp knife. Then after da deed is done, he washes said knife real good and puts it back in a drawer. Bingo. No prints, no murder weapon. Guy flushes his rubber gloves down da toilet an he's outta there, clean and tidy."

Spike saw me lookin' blankly at him.

"Hypo-thetically speakin', of course," he said.

"Of course. So he wouldn't get caught goin' in the house with a weapon."

"He gets less time in da joint if he's caught breakin' in."

It sounded smart, but I'd heard somethin' similar to that before. I wondered if Spike had. "You ever heard of the Boulder Bandit?"

Spike shrugged. "Him? He's a punk. Guy does one job a month? Gimme a break."

"It sounds like the killer used his method of breaking in. The Boulder Bandit doesn't bring burglary tools with him, he uses a rock from the yard to break in so he won't get caught with tools."

Spike seemed insulted by the idea of it. "Dat's so crude. Guy can't jimmy a window? What kinda punk burglars you got out heah? No self-respectin' second-story man I know would ever disgrace himself like that."

135

"The police think he did it. They already arrested him and charged him with murder."

"Local cops? They couldn't find a brick up their butt. They're just stickin' the job on some sap so they don't get heat from downtown."

"So who you think did it?"

Spike looked tired. "Like I said, dis is your problem, not mine. Remember our deal, Blackie. No Talkin.' "

He turned and went into his house.

EIGHTEEN

I left Spike's yard and trotted back down to my street, thinking our little talk was an important bit of information. It also narrowed the suspects to Bandit's human or Victor. It certainly wasn't Robert behind our house during the storm.

When I got to the corner intersection, I looked one way at my house and the other way toward the park. I decided to hit the park. I could get through the drainage ditch there and check the desert behind our house. Maybe I'd find smells or traces of the human from last night.

When I got there, it was empty except for quail families running across the grass. It was weird being at the park alone, without Meatloaf or any of the pack. Make that ex-pack, I guess. I stopped in the shade of a Palo Verde to cool down. The day-light was so hot I was beginning to think I'd misjudged the temperature. I thought I should have come out here first instead of going to Spike's place. But I was committed.

I went straight to the drainage pipe, then looked around for any humans watching me. Nothin'. Everyone was at work or inside their house. I ducked into the pipe and ran to the other side, comin' out in the bright day-light and the open desert.

The rain had already worked its magic. Dry grasses and wilted desert flowers stood taller. Dry bushes puffed up and came back from the dead. Insects buzzed and dived in the moist air, flittin' from plant to plant.

The ground was still damp, hopefully it was damp enough to find footprints. I wanted to know if someone actually was behind our house last night. I headed in the direction of our house, but I moved further out in the desert so Roxie or Bandit wouldn't catch sight of me. It wouldn't be hard to spot a black dog in the dried-out desert. Once away from the subdivision fence line, I found a hard, narrow path that took me in the direction of our house. It smelled faintly of coyote, but nothin' strong enough to be a recent scent. The rain last night had washed everything, so I couldn't be sure.

I stopped moving when I got near Bandit's place. I couldn't see any movement in his back yard, so I continued along slowly. I didn't need him makin' a racket at this point. Roxie didn't look like she was out either, but I doubted she'd bark at me. Then again, who knew things would turn out so bad for me in my own neighborhood.

The trail disappeared at a rain-washed gully. The sides were freshly cut and the bottom was full of fine dirt and sand runoff. I jumped down in it and scrambled up the other side, then continued on my way.

Ow!

I raised my paw in pain, I'd stepped on a cactus barb beside the trail. I sat and tried to pull it out with my teeth, but I couldn't reach it between my toes. It was one of those nasty double hedgehog needles. I had to leave it in and go on, limping with each step. It wouldn't be long, I was almost there.

Finally I was behind our house. There was no sign of Meatloaf, and that irritated me a little. I thought of barkin' to get him out, but I didn't want to alert the neighbor dogs. Especially Bandit.

I left the little trail and moved to the area where I'd seen something last night. I checked the ground carefully, but the desert floor here was fine broken granite, rocky and as hard as the sidewalk. I tried sniffing the bushes. Sniff, sniff. I could smell everything faintly, but nothing jumped out. The rain had washed the land of strong scents. I picked up Dominga and the smell of another coyote, but not the one who took Buffy.

I stopped and sat and tried again to get the needle out of my paw. I didn't have any better luck the second time. I was getting thirsty now, and wished I was home in the cool house with Meatloaf. But I got up and kept lookin'. I tried searching closer to our house, that's when I saw a footprint. It was half a print, a boot heel. But not a cowboy boot, it seemed more like a work boot or a hiking boot with those wiggly lines. I sniffed it. It smelled most strongly like the grass from our park. Maybe someone walked or ran through the park and jumped over the low fence there. The footprint itself was faint, washed and eroded from the night's hard rain.

It was hard to tell if this was an old impression or one from last night destroyed by all the water. I wished I'd paid more attention to my Blood Hound gifts. I should be better at finding things in the wild, instead of being a lazy house dog. This adventure gave me new admiration for Dominga living off the land like she did.

I went back and forth behind our house, sniffing and searching carefully for any other prints or signs of a human. I saw some indentations, but the ground was too rocky to be sure about anything except the one boot heel-print. I wouldn't call it definite proof, but it seemed to me someone was there last night.

It was hotter now and I was panting pretty good, so I thought I'd better get home while I was still able to walk. I made my way back to the trail and limped in the direction of the park. I winced with each step and just wanted to be home. When I came to the washed out gully, I couldn't jump down because my paw hurt too bad.

I limped up toward the mountains until I found an easier way down into the wash. Just before I stepped on the sand, I noticed coyote tracks in that part of the gully. These were fresh tracks, put down after last night's rain, maybe from this morning. I stuck my nose up to check. Yes. Coyote scent hung throughout the wet air, it was the same coyote scent I'd picked up behind our house, but stronger. I looked up and down the wash and crossed over, wary now. I jerked back when a rabbit leaped out from under a brittlebrush and zipped right by me. I didn't look twice at it, I kept movin' toward the park, more concerned at the moment about my own predators.

The trail kept goin' past our subdivision, so I left it and walked among the dry brush and desert trees. The gnarly Palo Verdes were bent over and hugging the desert floor, not trimmed and thinned like the desert trees in our neighborhood yards. These low-hanging branches made a good spot for animal lairs or hiding places, so I was cautious and I stayed away from these dense areas, limpin' slow but steady. The brush was also thick off the trail, sharp branches raked my coat as I squeezed between the creosote bushes. But I was making good time, it looked like I would make it out of there yet. I couldn't wait to get back to the security of my home, I was overheated and dying for a drink of cool water.

Everything changed with a flash of fear. I froze in my tracks, hyper-alert as a blast of raw coyote scent invaded my nose. The hair on my back rose and an ancient warning sense snapped me hyper alert. I crouched involuntarily and peered through the dense brush. There was no doubt what was happening now.

I was being hunted.

NINETEEN

Meatloaf yawned and stretched from his sleep. He wasn't sure what time it was, but his stomach was growling. Usually that meant it was halfway to second meal. He heard the TV in the next room, so he got up and wandered in to see what Taser was watching.

"Taser?"

When nobody answered, Meatloaf figured his partner must be in the yard, so he went outside to nose around. First he went out on the grass for a little business, then he checked all sides of the house. No Taser. When he went in the side yard, he noticed the gate was cracked open. This was unusual, he knew Robert wouldn't leave it open. He thought the meter-human must have come in the backyard to check something and got sloppy.

Meatloaf went inside the house and looked in the bathroom, because sometimes they slept by the toilet where it was coldest. Nope, Taser wasn't there, either. That left the upstairs, and he wasn't happy about going up there, he hated getting in trouble. So he lay down and waited, hoping to hear something that would give him a clue. When his eyelids started drooping, he forced himself to sit up and stay awake.

Well, catcrap.

He figured he had to go upstairs and look, he was worried something was wrong. Meatloaf scrambled up the stairs and went first to Robert and Judy's big room. Taser wasn't in there, but he thought he'd nose around. He sniffed around the bed, then he went in the bathroom where the smells were better. He nosed around in the closet and found the source—the dirty clothes basket. Meatloaf stuck his nose in there and checked for goodies.

Excellent.

He bit something black, pulled it out and dropped it on the floor. It was a pair of Judy's black panties. She always wore the same thing, little black panties. He'd seen them when she did the washing machine, but he couldn't get a pair without her catching him. He forgot all about Taser now, panties were his favorite thing.

He lay down and held them between his paws, but just before he started chewing, he remembered. This is how he lost his last human, chewing up her favorite panties. But Judy had so many, she wouldn't miss one pair, surely. He thought about it some more, then he got up and put them back in the clothes basket. He wasn't ready for a new human yet.

He went over to the bedroom windows and looked out the rear, but he didn't see anything unusual behind their house. So he went in Robert's airplane room. The smell of paint and glue was strong in there, but he knew not to eat anything. He looked out the side window. He could see a little bit of Nelly's backyard, more of Roxie's yard and a lot of Harley's place next door. The Rottweiler had his chew toys scattered all over the backyard grass.

Meatloaf was just about to leave when he noticed Harley himself, staring back at him from his house next door. He was in the upstairs bedroom too, looking out the side window just like Meatloaf. The two dogs nodded at each other, they'd never talked much besides saying hello. And since Harley never came to the park, they really never got to know him. Too bad, Meatloaf thought, maybe Harley knew what was happening around here.

He cocked his head. Maybe Harley knew where Taser was right now. Woof!

Meatloaf barked at him, then motioned with his nose at the back fence.

Woof, woof.

Harley barked back.

Meatloaf ran downstairs and out to their common backyard fence. He wouldn't be able to see Harley, but he thought they could talk through the open bars of their rear view fence.

"Harley, it's Meatloaf."

"Yo, Jack. Wassup?"

Meatloaf could hear him fine. "I'm looking for Taser, you seen him today?"

"Yeah, dog walked by my house a while ago, headin' for the park."

"You sure?"

"I know a brother when I see one. Dog's crazy, too hot outside for us mutts."

"I hear you." Meatloaf thought that was weird, he didn't see why Meatloaf would leave without telling him. And why would he go to the park? He figured Taser must be upset. "Hey Harley, how come you don't come to the park at night with us? Everybody else does."

"My dumb-butt humans won't let me out. Ever since I bit some pup- human and they got sued, they keep me locked in the house. Weren't my fault, I hadda bite him."

"Biting's death penalty stuff, you know. Dogs aren't supposed to bite."

"Yeah, why you think they gave us teeth? Kid hit me with a nine iron. I look like a golf ball to you, Jack?"

"It's Meatloaf, actually." Meatloaf didn't say any more about the biting, but he thought Harley must have anger-management problems. "Hey, you know what's been going on around here, don't you? All this commotion?"

"Straight up. That party-girl down the street gots herself killed. I seen all them cops over there. I seen her dead body come out, too. Loaded her up in a wagon and took her away."

He should have known Harley would know something. Too bad they didn't ask him about the murder before. "You see anything else funny? We're trying to figure out who killed her. The police-humans arrested a guy, but Taser thinks it's someone from the neighborhood."

Harley snorted. "Tell you what, it be someone 'round here, I know who."

"Come on."

"It's true. You know Roxie, other side of me? I think her master did the deed."

"Roxie's human? That's impossible."

Harley sounded insulted. "Don't be telling me my business, Jack. I been watchin' this hood for years. I know what's goin' down around here."

"Why would Roxie's male kill her?"

"She dumped his butt for another stud."

"Who?"

"Roxie's male. You listening over there, Jack?"

Meatloaf was confused. "No, who did Vicki dump him for?"

"Who's Vicki?"

"Vicki's the female that got murdered. Who'd she dump Roxie's human for?"

"Bandit's male. See, this Vicki girl was in some serious heat. Roxie's male be over there all the time. I seen them mountin' in the back yard, mountin' in the swimmin' pool, mountin' on the furniture. Then one day he's gone and it be Bandit's male's checkin' her plumbing. I figure he got up-set."

"Who was upset, mount-ee number one or mount-ee number two?

Now Harley was confused. "Whatchu talking about? Mount-ee what?"

Meatloaf explained. "We're trying to be consistent in our investigation terminology. The human doing the mounting is the mount-er. The one being mounted is the mount-ee."

"Listen Jack, that don't make no difference to this girl. Sometimes she be the mount-ee and sometimes she be the mount-er. You shoulda seen them goin' at it in the swimmin pool. I thought she was gonna drown that sucker."

144

This was important information. He wondered why Roxie hadn't told the pack about this, she'd have known what was going on, she lived right next door. It seemed like everyone had something to hide around here.

Then Meatloaf remembered.

"Did you happen to hear anything out back the night it rained? Taser said he saw a human in the desert behind our house."

"I knew it! Everybody thinks I'm a nut, but I saw a guy. Big dude, sneakin' around the bushes. I barked like the house was on fire, least until my master yelled at me. He don't like it much when I wake him up."

Meatloaf wasn't sure if this confirmation was good news or bad.

"Thanks for the help, Harley, but just for the record, my name is Meatloaf, not Jack."

"I know yo' name is Meatloaf."

"But you called me Jack."

"Look. Everyone is Jack to me. That's just what it is."

This made no sense at all, he thought maybe Harley had too many issues. "Thanks again, I'll tell all this to Taser when he comes back."

"You do that. Be cool."

Meatloaf went back in their house at sat, waiting for his buddy to show up. He didn't want to say anything to Harley about it, but he was getting really worried.

TWENTY

The coyote scent grew stronger but I still couldn't see him. I looked behind and to either side. Nothing. I waited, still crouching, thinking I was hidden as well as he. Finally I decided I had to move. I took a few slow steps forward until I could see the park fence, but the path to it was full of dense brush. The smell of Buffy's killer was everywhere, it looked like he'd come back for another easy victim. With each step I checked the brush for the big grey.

Where was he?

I had to get out of there, I wasn't in shape for a fight today. I started limping as fast as I could with my sore paw, but running was out of the question, it hurt too bad. I dodged big bushes and overgrown trees, trying to stay out in the open. I got on a little open trail and felt better about my chances. I started to think of Robert for some reason, and all of a sudden I missed his kind words and affection.

Wait.

The coyote smell was intense, he had to be near. I turned a full circle, peering carefully through the creosote. Still nothing. He blended well in this landscape, he was probably hugging the ground, waiting to pounce. I moved slower and looked carefully until I was close enough to the park to see the drainage pipe exit. I started to relax, thinking I'd made it to safety after all.

Then I saw him.

Buffy's killer was standing between me and the drainage pipe. He didn't flinch, he didn't seem afraid of me or any other living thing. His head hung low, his yellow eyes stared coldly through me. I stood my ground and prepared myself for a fight, it was my only option now.

146

My fear slowly melted, replaced by anger at what he'd done to Buffy. If someone was gonna die today, it was gonna be this creature. This was the animal that took a friend's life and threatened my neighborhood. I moved a few steps closer, trying not to show weakness by limping.

I wasn't afraid of fighting this animal, I weighed twice what he did, I had the fight advantage. I curled my lip and growled. Immediately I heard growling in response—deep, menacing growling.

But this growling came from behind me. I spun around, wide-eyed at a new threat. Crouched to my rear was a second male coyote, fangs bared. My advantage was gone.

TWENTY-ONE

When Robert got home from work, Meatloaf was waiting at the door alone. Robert looked in the kitchen for Taser, then he went upstairs to change his clothes like he did every day after work. It wasn't until he came downstairs that he asked about the missing black dog.

Meatloaf, where's Taser? It's time to eat.

Robert went in the pantry, put dog food in both bowls and then added a little water. When he turned around from the sink he had a bowl in each hand and a quizzical look on his face.

Taser?

He called out in the house, but got no response. Robert set Meatloaf's bowl down and went outside to look for his missing Labrador. Meatloaf ignored his food and followed along, a detail that struck Robert as very unusual. Robert walked out back and checked the yard. No Taser. Meatloaf went over to the side yard and stared at the gate.

Woof.

Robert followed as Meatloaf led him to the side gate. He saw it was open, so he went out in the front yard to search, his Lab right on his heels. He went to the front porch, then to the far side of the house. He tried calling out in the neighborhood.

Taser!

Robert put his hands on his hips and looked at Meatlaof.

If only you guys could talk.

He got down on his knees and spoke directly to his pet.

Meatloaf, where's Taser? Get Taser.

148

Meatloaf left the yard and took off trotting for the park. Robert watched for a second, then followed after him. Meatloaf made a beeline for the park, ignoring the barks of neighborhood dogs watching from their yards. Robert jogged behind until he caught him in the middle of the park. He tried calling again.

Taser!

Meatloaf put his nose down and followed it to the big drain pipe. Robert peered inside, then looked at dog prints in the mud leading into the pipe. He bent down and looked closer. He could see the muddy prints go into the pipe, but he couldn't see any prints showing Taser had come out.

He stared past the desert to the mountains and called again. Meatloaf watched impatiently, it was obvious to him Taser had gone to the other side, why didn't his master just go over there. They were wasting too much time.

Robert finally went to the park's fence gate and fiddled with the latch. It looked like it was difficult to open, but he figured it out and went on through. Robert checked the little trail while Meatloaf sniffed all around. He found lots of strange scents mixed with Taser's scent.

Find Taser, Meatloaf. Where is he?

Meatloaf followed his nose up the trail, making little side trips into the desert that didn't pan out. He turned around and came back, looked up at Robert and whined sadly. There were too-many scents.

No? Keep looking, boy, follow me.

Robert threaded his way through the desert brush as Meatloaf followed close behind, sniffing bushes. He walked in a widening arc, studying the desert floor for clues. Every now and then Meatloaf would sniff the ground, but he never reacted much until they got to an open area where the ground was torn up and disturbed. This was it. He barked and sniffed all around, then he growled at an invisible foe. The smell of coyote was so strong it scared him.

Robert bent down and studied the earth. He found small patches of fresh blood, one large red spot even had black hairs matted in it.

149

Meatloaf sniffed as Robert looked. The desert gravel was scratched and raked, it definitely looked like a fight of some sort happened right there.

Suddenly Meatloaf got up and sniffed the air, then pointed off the trail, whining loudly.

What is it, boy?

Robert walked over and found the lifeless form laying under a bush. He poked it cautiously with his toe.

Woof Woof Woof Woof!

Quiet!

It was obvious this coyote had died in the fight, Robert thought it had to be Taser's work.

Meatloaf whined repeatedly. If Taser had killed this coyote, where had he gone to? Could he be laying under a bush somewhere, confused and injured?

If Taser was hurt there wasn't much time left for him to survive in this heat. They searched a larger area, moving quickly in an ever widening circle. But now they were looking for a black dog lying prone, fighting for his life—or lifeless.

TWENTY-TWO

I backed away from the second coyote, my mind racing with fear, thinking now of escape. But I knew there was no escape for me, I'd need to fight them both.

I'd wait until they got close enough to attack, then I'd battle one at a time and hope the other didn't disable me. I was so wired for the fight now, I couldn't feel any pain from the needle in my paw. My vision narrowed to the immediate threat, all I could see was coyotes. No desert. No sky. Just snarling coyotes.

They took cautious but deliberate steps toward me, acting like they weren't scared of me or a fight. I could tell they weren't gonna back off until they had me. As much as I wanted to fight the one who took Buffy, I planned to hit the other coyote first. He was probably starving and weaker. I knew the big male had eaten yesterday.

I backed up off the trail so I could see both coyotes. Here the daylight glared in my eyes. I tried to maneuver them so the advantage would be mine, but they were intent on jumping me any moment. I tensed in anticipation, my ears flat to my head, my lips curled.

If there was anything I learned in the pound, it was once a fight was inevitable, waiting only gave the edge to your opponent. I wasn't gonna wait any longer. When the second coyote got within two lengths, I sprung at him.

He was expecting it, he sidestepped me and slashed my shoulder with his teeth. I winced but didn't cry out. I spun away from both of them and we faced-off again. Now the first big male advanced at me, teeth bared.

151

He jumped forward and leaped back before I knew what happened, slicing my lip open. I flashed with anger and launched my full weight at him, pushing hard, trying desperately to force him on his back.

He was too fast for my clumsy move, he retreated far enough that I couldn't follow him, I couldn't let the other male get behind me. I stopped attacking to rethink my adversaries. These were not domestic dogs in the protected confines of the pound. They were a new opponent for me, a tough-breed born fighting for survival, not pampered and spoiled from birth. I moved now only to keep them off me while I tried to get my wind.

We circled each other as I probed for advantage, but they had it all, I could only fend off their moves.

They came at me again.

Fangs bared, they took turns leaping and slashing, then jumping back out of reach. It was a tactic I couldn't defend myself from, I was cut and bleeding and growing weaker. I had to go on the attack soon or it would be too late. I couldn't run, I wouldn't make the park before they pulled me down. They had speed and aggression, I had muscle and mass. I had to use my weight advantage or I was gonna die right there.

I lunged at the big male's head, but faked at the last minute, turning and hitting his side with all my weight. He tumbled backward off the trail, but I let him go and spun around. My second attacker was almost on me. I bit down hard on his muzzle, he jerked but I wouldn't let him go, I clamped down even harder and pushed back, twisting my jaws and cutting him deep. When I did release him he escaped to the side, shaking his head.

I didn't wait, I knew what was coming. When I flipped around, Buffy's killer was three-lengths away. I hit him low and hard, my rear legs thrusting desperately with all their failing strength. This time he lost his footing completely and fell.

It had to be now.

I leaped on his throat and bit deep as he kicked frantically. As his soft throat yielded to my grip, I clamped harder and harder with newfound strength. He gurgled and kicked, but the kicks grew weaker and weaker as his breath left him. Finally, he didn't move at all.

But one threat remained.

I looked back to where the other coyote had been, he was still there, not moving, just staring. His muzzle was bloody from the fight, I thought he was still dazed. I moved back on the trail and took two steps toward him, then I stopped. It wasn't his muzzle wound that halted his attack, something else was wrong. He wasn't looking at me, he was looking at something behind me. Suddenly he dashed up the trail toward the mountain.

Senses heightened, I turned around and saw why.

It was a man with a club raised to strike.

TWENTY-THREE

It seemed to Meatloaf they'd been searching a long time when Robert finally quit and walked back to the park. They stood together on the grass, looking one last time at the desert that had swallowed Taser. Then they slowly walked home.

Meatloaf lay by the water dish for a long time, drinking and resting. Robert filled it twice. The bowl of dog food was still sitting there untouched, he still wasn't hungry. Robert didn't seem hungry either. He sat at the kitchen table and looked out the back window, drinking his own water from a glass.

Finally Robert got up and made a sandwich. He ate it standing outside by the back fence, staring out at the desert. Meatloaf wandered over to his food bowl and ate half of it. Then Robert came in because it was getting dark outside.

Let's go to the park, Robert said.

Meatloaf didn't move.

Come on, you can see your friends.

Meatloaf was too tired, but he thought it might do Robert some good to talk to other humans. So they went out. It didn't seem the same without his buddy there. If Taser was with him, he would grill Roxie on the facts she kept hidden from the pack. That meant Meatloaf was going to have to ask the tough questions, which made him uncomfortable. He hated confrontation.

But he'd do it. For Taser.

When they got there, Robert stood with the other males and females and talked, probably asking if anyone knew anything. Meatloaf saw

Gizmo and Roxie, so he went over to them. They were a little out of breath from running around, but they also acted cool to him.

Gizmo spoke first. "Where's Taser? He scared to come to the park? Too scared to take his medicine?"

Meatloaf wasn't going to let them make him angry. "He's missing. We don't know where he is, but we know he got in a fight with a coyote on the other side of the fence." He pointed. "Over there in the desert."

Winston the Bulldog showed up and Roxie filled him in. Winston thought it was serious. "Bloody hell! Is he all right?"

"I don't know how Taser is, but the coyote he fought is dead."

"Dead!"

"I bet he went up there to kill it," Gizmo said. "That dog has some guts. He probably knew he had to redeem himself by killing the beast."

"That must have been some fight," Winston said.

"Was it the grey that got Buffy?" Roxie asked.

"I couldn't tell for sure, but I think it was."

"I wonder why Taser didn't come home?" Winston asked.

Meatloaf shrugged. "We don't know, that's why I'm worried."

"I saw you and Robert walk by earlier," said Roxie. "Is that what you were doing, looking for Taser?"

"Yeah. We found some blood from Taser and then we found the dead coyote. We looked everywhere in the area for him but no luck. I'd pick up his scent for a while but then it would disappear."

Gizmo looked serious. "Wow, dog. That's not good. It's too hot up there to survive very long. Maybe we should go look ourselves."

"Thanks, but I think we covered every tree and bush all the way up to the mountain. I'm hoping he'll show up late tonight, but…" He looked down at the grass.

"He didn't say anything? You didn't talk to him this morning?"

Meatloaf shook his head. "He slipped out after breakfast. He must have left the house when I was sleeping, I didn't see him leave. When I talked to Harley next door, he said Taser walked toward the park. But he didn't come back."

"Bad break."

"Any of you see him today?"

Nobody had.

Winston seemed lost in thought. "Very strange. I don't think I've ever heard of a case of canine suicide."

"What's wrong with you, he didn't commit suicide," Meatloaf said. "He just left home."

"Maybe he ran away before Robert puts you guys in the pound."

"Like a bail jumper," said Winston.

Meatloaf was beginning to regret coming to the park. These guys were all over the place. "You know, he still wants to find that killer. He's convinced someone local human did it. He probably went out this morning to investigate."

Roxie scoffed. "That's crazy. The police already arrested the guy who did. Taser is just trying to redeem himself."

Meatloaf wasn't going to drop it. "But the police haven't interviewed all the witnesses."

"Like who," said Gizmo. "The coyote mother?"

"Like Harley, my neighbor."

They snickered at the mention of the Rottweiler.

"I don't think Harley is a credible witness," said Winston. "He's a nutter."

"Not true," said Meatloaf. "I talked to him today, he's got some issues, but he's not crazy. He watches the neighborhood and he knows what goes on."

"You telling us he saw the killer?" asked Roxie.

"No. Well, maybe. One thing he saw was Bandit's male slipping next door to mount Vicki. He went into a lot of detail."

Winston got animated. "Ha! Sorry I missed it. Taser was right about that, I always knew he was right."

"So what," said Roxie. "That doesn't mean anything."

"No? How about the fact that he saw your male over there mounting Vicki? Does that mean something?"

Everyone looked at Roxie.

She looked down at her paws. "Ahh, look guys. I knew he was a Vicki mount-er, but it doesn't make any difference. He didn't kill her, he had no reason to."

Winston looked mad. "That's not for you to decide. Withholding evidence from our investigation? Outrageous."

Meatloaf continued. "Harley said he was over there a lot. With him being involved with her so much, You'd think he'd be an important suspect."

"Why couldn't he be guilty?" Gizmo asked.

"Because I didn't hear him leave the house the night of the murder," Roxie said. "I heard the howl that night, I was outside, I heard what was going on. I would have smelled him over at Vicki's."

Meatloaf objected. "You said it was too windy that night to smell what was happening next door. You said all you smelled was creosote bush off the desert."

"OK, I said that. But he was home, I would've known if he left."

"You sure? Maybe he left while you were outside. For someone to murder another human, he'd have to be very sneaky."

"You're just trying to stick-up for Taser. You're trying to blame me because he screwed up."

Meatloaf shook his head. "We're just looking for the truth."

"That's right," said Winston. "All we want is a proper investigation."

"It doesn't matter now," Roxie said. "The police have their suspect and Victor is leaving the neighborhood."

"Leaving?"

"My humans heard he's selling the house and not coming back, right after the funeral on Friday. It's kind of his going-away affair, that's why all the neighbors are coming."

That concerned Meatloaf. "But he's a suspect. Once he leaves, it's over."

"Let the man find some peace," said Winston. "So sorry, but I've dilly-dallied too long. I hope you find Taser."

He ran off while the other two went out in the park, leaving Meatloaf to sniff bushes. He wandered around a while, looking across the fence for any sign of his friend. He started to whine, then he caught himself. He had to be strong, now.

Meatloaf glanced over at Robert, he was talking intently with Gizmo's humans. Someone must have seen Tazor walking through the neighborhood. But Gizmo lived in the other direction from the park, so they likely wouldn't have seen him.

He checked the park. No dogs were anywhere near the drainage pipe, but one of the male humans was standing guard down there with a golf club. They didn't want any more coyotes taking pets, for sure.

Bandit was out there following Simba around. She seemed polite with him, but Meatloaf couldn't pick up any more than that. Still, it didn't seem right, she shouldn't be hanging around with that Weimaraner. She probably needs her ego stroked. Taser should have listened to him, he told him Goldens were high-maintenance dogs.

Finally Robert called and they went home. Robert jogged to the house but Meatloaf lagged behind because he didn't feel like any more exercise. When he got back, he lay at Robert's feet in the TV room, sleeping and dreaming of better days with his friend. Robert had the TV on but no sound. He wasn't even watching the picture, he was just staring at the wall. When it got late, Robert got down and gave him a hug and a dog bone before going upstairs.

Meatloaf sat alone in the living room with his dog bone, thinking what Taser might do next. He needed his partner's brains and strength right now. Then it came to him.

Meatloaf got up and went out back to confront Dominga

TWENTY-FOUR

I froze, unsure of my next move.

The strange man held the club over his head and watched the coyote run up the trail. Slowly he lowered it, then he dropped it on the ground. For a moment I thought of attacking this two-legged menace, all I saw was a threat, I didn't care if it was human or not.

He was wearing heavy gloves and a grey shirt and pants. He approached me slowly, speaking calmly, saying reassuring words I could not understand. I could barely hear, I was still in fight mode and not trusting anything but my ancient senses.

Slowly it came back as the hot desert returned. One coyote was dead, one was gone. I began to relax, even in this strange human's presence.

He bent down and checked my wounds, talking to me the whole time. I was cut and bleeding in different places, but my shoulder was bleeding the worst. I didn't feel pain there or anywhere, I was numb all over my body. I let him pick me up, he spoke so soothingly I wasn't scared at all. He carried me up to the park fence and through a gate I didn't even know was there.

He put me down in the shade of a tree and went over to his truck. Somehow I wasn't scared, I knew I needed human help now that the fight was over. I lay there licking my wounds until he returned with some water in a round plastic dish. I drank some and rested, drank some and rested. Now my body was aching from the battle, all my muscles were sore. I was older since my dog-fighting days, I wasn't in the shape I remembered.

He washed my wounds with cold water and a rag, pretty soon the bleeding stopped, but then everything started to hurt. He put some spray stuff on them and that helped. Then he checked me all over, feeling my bones. He even found the cactus needle in my paw and pulled it out with pliers or something. I thought he must be a human doctor or a vet from our little neighborhood, someone out jogging in the desert. I was lucky he came to help, I realized I needed him.

As he worked on me, I thought of Meatloaf and what he must be thinking. I should have told him what I was up to, he was probably worried. On the other hand, Meatloaf never seemed to worry about anything, it was like he didn't care as much as I did.

The man stood up and talked into a radio or a telephone, saying stuff I couldn't hear or understand. I put my head down and rested, I was so exhausted I couldn't keep my head up. When he was through talking, he picked me up and took me to his truck. I was glad I had a ride home, I didn't want to walk, I just wanted to rest. I didn't care about the murder in our neighborhood right now, I didn't have the energy to deal with it.

His truck had compartments like a construction truck, only after he put me in one did I realize something was wrong. This truck smelled of different dogs and cats, I even smelled a dead skunk. I thought it was a vet's truck, but when he drove out of our subdivision toward the big road, I realized the awful truth.

I'd been too trusting. This wasn't a nice vet or doctor after all. He was an animal-control human. All my efforts were wasted, the thing I feared most was happening anyway. I was going to the dog pound.

TWENTY-FIVE

The pound was exactly as I remembered—same building, same noise, same smell—only the humans were different. They put me in a small cage not far from the one where I spent much of my last visit.

From what I could see, all the dogs were new, I didn't recognize anyone. Even Mad Marmaduke was gone. I wondered about Major, if he really did die in this stinking place, old and alone like he feared. I put my head down and tried not to think about it.

A friendly Vet-human had washed me and patched up my cuts and shoulder wound as soon as I came in. That was one good thing. Now I was sportin' a fresh bandage and a clean coat. Whatever they'd done helped a lot, but now I was exhausted, so I closed my eyes and slept deeply in spite of the noise from the other cages.

I got up when the guards started bringin' round the food in my section. One by one the doors opened and a bowl of somethin' grey and lumpy slid in. I sniffed it, but it smelled old so I walked away. I wasn't very hungry anyway.

"I know it stinks," someone said. "But you better eat it, you won't get much food while you're here."

I looked over at the cage next to me, I saw a salt and pepper Border Collie smiling back. He repeated his warning.

"Eat up, my friend—even if you're not hungry. They don't give you much and you'll lose half of that."

He nodded at me.

"Name's Dakota. This your first time?"

I moved closer to the bars. My cage neighbor was about an inch taller than me, but thinner, less stocky. He seemed nice. It was good to see a friendly muzzle.

"I'm Taser, I been in before. I did a long stretch a while back, seems like forever now."

"I been in before, too. I tell you, the place has changed, it's gone downhill bad."

I looked around the building, I wasn't sure what he was talkin' about, the pound seemed the same to me. I think the Vet-human was the same one that was here when I was, but the guards were new. Maybe that was it.

"How long you been here?" I asked him.

"It's been a while. My human is in jail, drunk driving. He's got a problem with drinking. This is my third time in here while he sits in jail."

"That's tough."

"It's not so bad, he's a good guy. He'll come and get me when he gets out. He does landscape work in town and makes good money. Where did you live?"

I cringed when he said 'did'. "I live up north, in Scottsdale."

He nodded. "Yeah, we do work up there, that's where the money is. There's a lot of rich out-of-town buyers overpay for stuff. When my human gets paid at the end of a job he goes on a binge, sometimes he gets arrested. They take him to the drunk tank and me to the pound."

"You ride with him all the time?"

"Yep. In the front seat of his truck, I help him landscape."

I felt sorry for Dakota getting thrown back in here all the time. "You must be an expert on the pound then."

"I know how to survive, if that's what you mean."

I nosed in a guard's direction. "How's the screws? They give you any trouble?"

"Nah, they're fine. It's the packs that make things miserable."

"What packs? In here?"

162

"There's two packs now, they run the place like it was their own. You got the Blacks and the Browns. If you're not lucky enough to be in one or the other you're an Outcast."

"That's crazy, they didn't have packs when I was here last."

"You were lucky. Phoenix is a big city now. Blacks came in from Chicago, the Browns are an L.A. pack. They infiltrated the Pound and now the screws can't get 'em out. Besides, I don't think they really want to, because the packs keep everyone in line."

I looked at Dakota's coat, it was an even mix of black and white. "So what pack you in?"

"Neither."

That surprised me. "Most dogs are mixed color, so who decides which pack you're in?"

He thought. "Well, you're all black, but that doesn't mean you're automatically in the Black pack. It just means you qualify to be asked to join, if you meet their pack requirements."

"Like what?"

"Special talents, skills."

"I'd rather go my own way, thanks. I never was much good at taking orders from other dogs."

Dakota hesitated. "Well, that may not be smart. You might need them for protection."

"Protection? From what?"

"From the other pack. Plus, if you don't get in a pack, you end up in the Outcasts, they're the dregs of pound society. You have to give half your food to the packs."

"No way."

"It's true. You can only eat half your food, you have to leave the rest in your bowl. Then one of the pack members comes and eats the rest. It keeps them stronger than the rest of us."

I looked at the bowl in his cage, only half the food was gone. The rest just sat there.

"So you're an Outcast?"

"Yep. I didn't get asked to join a pack. I think they only take so many so they can get more food."

"That's Catcrap. I'm not puttin' up with that." I nosed my bowl over close to the bars and tipped it over. "Here. Eat my meal. I don't need it."

Dakota looked around to see if anyone was watching us. "I don't know."

"Eat it, don't be crazy."

He ate hungrily at my spilt-bowl contents while I pushed the last food through the bars with my nose. I didn't care what had changed around here, no one was gonna force me to join their pack. I didn't survive the last five tough years to be under some mutt's paw.

I watched Dakota eat the last bits, thinking it wasn't gonna get any easier for me. I stretched my sore muscles to keep them limber. It looked like I wasn't through fightin' yet.

TWENTY-SIX

Meatloaf went right out to the fence and waited. It was a weak nightlight, but he could see pretty well in the dark, so he watched the brush for Dominga's slight shadow. He wondered if Taser could be out there. If he was, Dominga would know. She would also know if he was dead.

Meatloaf rarely got angry, but he was upset at this marauding bunch of coyotes tonight. What right did they have to kill and take what they wanted? He knew he wouldn't kill another animal to survive. These coyotes should just be nice to humans, join the dog family and stop this nonsense of eating their friends.

He shivered. What if coyotes had eaten Taser? What if Dominga had eaten him? He tried to put it out of his mind.

"Who are you?"

Meatloaf jumped, she'd appeared out of nowhere. Dominga stared at him through the metal fence bars like he was some strange creature. Meatloaf was speechless, so she asked the question again.

"Who are you, Taser's friend?" Her tone was hostile, unfriendly.

Meatloaf was unnerved by her commanding presence. He was too scared to be mad anymore. "Yes, his friend. Where is he? What happened up there?"

"He went where fat dogs should not go. He went to Tajo's hunting grounds."

"Tajo?"

"The one who took your small dog. Tajo is a powerful hunter, but Taser killed him in a fierce battle. He fought both Tajo and Salvador.

"You're saying he fought two coyotes?"

165

"He was very lucky."

Meatloaf thought this was funny. "What luck? He won the fight."

"It is true, your friend is a strong fighter."

Meatloaf stared at her. "Why do you kill us? We're brother animals, we just want to be friends."

"It is easy to be friends when your belly is full. Look at your fat body, are you ever hungry?"

He thought about that. "All the time."

"Then you are spoiled. If you had to hunt your dinner, you would eat us, too. There are no friends when you are starving to death, when your small ones are starving."

Meatloaf was nauseous at the thought of eating a coyote. Even with barbeque sauce.

"Where is my friend? Is Taser still alive?"

"A man took him away. Salvador said after the fight, a man came and helped your friend. He watched them from a hill."

"What man?"

"I do not know. He has chased us before. He protects this land with his machine. He moves from place to place, chasing us away from our prey."

"The machine moves?"

"Yes.

"Is the machine big, did the man go inside it?"

"Yes."

"And Taser?"

"He put your friend inside."

Animal Control humans.

"Where'd they go, did he see?"

"They went down the mountain, away from this place." She looked at the bone sitting on the fence between them but didn't say anything about it. She didn't act hostile anymore.

Meatloaf wasn't mad at her either. "I'm sorry about Tajo."

166

"Tajo was wrong to attack your friend. We hold no grudge against any of you, but we must kill to survive."

"Why us? Why not stick to rabbits and cats? If you want, I can show you all the houses where the cats live."

She didn't seem interested.

"I will make no promise for our kind. I only know this, spoiled one. Taser was a good friend to me, so I am sad he is hurt."

"He's hurt?" Meatloaf raised his voice. "What's wrong with him?"

"His leg, hurt from the fight. Don't worry, your friend is very strong. We have much respect for him."

Meatloaf saw her eye the bone again. "Please, take it. Thank you for helping. I'm afraid Taser is gone, we won't see him again."

She didn't move. "He will come back. You will see."

Meatloaf shook his head. "You don't understand. The humans took him to the dog prison. They locked him up, he's gone for good."

"Why do you give up so easy? Are you lazy too?"

"These are special Animal Control people, like the police-humans. They took him away to a different city and put him in a metal cage."

She didn't seem fazed by this.

"Yes, yes. But you are a dog. Use your human to get him back."

"I can't do that, I can't talk to them. I can't tell then what to do."

That gave her pause.

"I do not understand. They tell you what to do, yes?"

"Yes."

"But you can not tell them what you want?"

"No. See, we can talk to dogs or coyotes, but humans don't understand our words. We know some of their words, but they don't know any of ours."

She scoffed. "That makes you slaves to them."

"Not slaves. Companions, friends. They help us and we do things for them. We get love and food and a house to live in. They get love and protection and, and ..." He tried to think of something else. "And dog poop."

167

"If they cannot help you," she said, "It is up to you alone to save your friend."

"Me? How can I save him? I can't drive, I can't find out where he is."

She shook her head. "Listen to your talk. You are weak. You must get out, go to the city find your friend. Use your brain."

"I don't know, my brain is not that good. I'm from California."

"You cry like small one. Be strong fighter like your friend. Get up, go! Your friend would come for you."

She was right. Taser would come to save him.

He sat very straight. "I'll do it. I'll go find Taser."

With that assurance, Dominga took the bone and ran out toward the mountains.

TWENTY-SEVEN

It wasn't too long after meal time that they started opening cage doors.

Clang.

Clang.

Clang.

You never get used to it, the noise sears your brain and puts your nerves on hard edge. It was a male guard who opened my door, he never even looked at me, he just went on to the next cage.

Clang.

Clang.

I followed Dakota out to the yard and did my business first thing. Other dogs scurried around, some running, some watching, some waiting. Barking came from all corners. I stuck close to Dakota, hoping to get the lay of the land from a recent veteran. He nudged me and pointed to a black Boxer in one corner.

"That's Digger, head of the Blacks. He's mean, careful not to piss him off."

I nodded and we kept walking. I noticed a couple dogs walking back into the cage area. One of them went in Dakota's cage.

"Hey, that mutt's in your house."

Dakota looked. "That's a pack dog. It's his turn to eat half of my food."

I couldn't believe it. "How many Outcasts are in here?"

"More than half the pound."

"Why don't you band together and stand up to these dogs? There's more of you than them."

Dakota shrugged. "Most of us are short-timers, we'll be out of here in a few days. The pack dogs are lifers. You might as well just give them your food to avoid the punishment."

I looked around and saw a group sitting around a brown and white Bull Terrier. He was short and wide, tough looking.

"Is that the Browns?"

"That's them. The Bull Terrier is Paco, he's the leader. Most of his dogs are phonies, lightweights. They act tough with Paco around to back them up. He's crazy, the toughest fighter in here, check out all his scars."

I started to look, but then I turned to see a commotion behind us. It looked like a group of Blacks had a Basset Hound surrounded and they were taking turns nipping him. He yelped at each little bite to his flank.

"See, the pack is punishing him for eating more than half of his food. He didn't leave what he was supposed to."

Dakota was right, this place had really gone downhill. I wondered if Robert would come to pick me up or if he'd leave me here like he planned anyway. The more I thought about it, the more I worried that he might not even know I was here.

Dakota nudged me in the ribs. "Look out. Here comes trouble."

I saw Digger and two Blacks ambling over to our spot along the wall. Most of the dogs in the yard stopped what they were doing and watched. The Boxer was tall, taller than his pack members and a lot taller than me. He walked right up to us and stopped. I could feel a strong alpha presence but I didn't give in to it. He looked at me but spoke to Dakota.

"Hey OC, who's da new dogmeat?"

I didn't wait for my friend to speak for me. I cocked my head and spoke up. "What's it to ya, Blackie?"

Dakota cringed.

Digger's head jerked back at my impudence, but then he laughed.

"Arf arf arf. Dat's rich." He looked at his bodyguards. "What's it to ya. Arf arf. Dis dog has cajones."

170

They chuckled along with their boss. The two of them looked like Dobermans mixed with somethin' heavy. They scared the poop outta me, but I wasn't gonna let on.

I looked 'em up and down. "And who are these guys, the Black and Blues Brothers?"

"Arf arf. You're killin' me, dogmeat. Hey, you know who I am, don't you kid? You need to join our pack. You're flying the right colors and you got attitude. We could use more attitude around here."

I stared at him but said nothing. There was something about him that struck me as unusual. He watched me, then finally asked.

"Well?"

"I'm still thinkin'." That struck him as funny, too.

"Arf arf arf. He's thinking. Join our pack kid, we won't ask you twice."

"What's in it for me?"

"Protection, for one. You get bennies, like extra food and entertainment. And you don't get your butt bit."

We looked over at the Basset Hound being punished. Digger seemed proud of his goons.

"See dat? A lot can go wrong in here. These brown dogs are vicious, you need our help to keep them off your back. You don't wanna end up in a Chicago Overcoat."

I wasn't sure how long I could be polite. "Browns? Those are Blacks beatin' up that dog."

"Da boys are just straightening out that Basset."

"That what you call the entertainment in here?"

"Dat hound was stealing from us."

"By eating his own food?"

Digger looked irritated. "It's our food. If you ain't one of us, you got to pay us protection, less somethin' unfortunate happens to ya. We need that food to stay stronger than da Browns."

"I appreciate your concern, but I get along pretty well on my own."

He looked me over. "That right. That why you got a big bandage on your leg?"

"You should see the other dog."

I thought I'd pushed him as far as he was gonna go.

"What you don't get, dogmeat, is you need us more then we need you."

Then he got ugly.

"Maybe you'd rather be our food-bitch, like Outcast here?" He swung his head in Dakota's direction. Dakota looked more than uncomfortable.

I'd had enough small talk. "Thanks, but I'll pass."

Digger didn't get it.

"What's that mean, dogmeat? Tell me straight."

"Go mount yourself. I'm not gonna be one of your goons."

Dakota let out a whimper and slumped to the floor in the submission position.

The Boxer looked furious, his cronies looked confused. They probably didn't get many turndowns, even less insults. I tensed for an attack over the diss, but the stare-down ended with a loud whistle from a pound guard. Yard exercise was over and it was time for cage lock-down.

"Next time we meet," Digger said to me, "You gonna need more bandages."

He backed off but the two Dobermans curled their lips and growled. I stayed there with Dakota until they moved across the floor to the cages in the front of the building.

Dakota finally looked up at me like I was an idiot. "What is wrong with you, dog? You got a death wish or something? That animal is gonna kill you."

I shook my head. "Remember what you said about the other pack leader, Paco?"

"I said he was nuts. I said he was a fighter."

"What'd you say about scars?"

"I told you to look at how many he had."

"That's right. He had a lot. How many scars did you see on Digger?"

"You're crazy, dog. I'm not talking to you anymore."

"No scars. Digger hasn't got one scar. He's all talk."

"You're insane."

"Dakota, listen. Nobody wants to feel pain. If Digger really thinks I'm gonna fight him, he's not gonna be anxious to mess with me. He's a cupcake, he doesn't want to get hurt."

"What about his pack? They'll go after you even if he doesn't."

"Maybe. But all these mutts respect is strength, I'm gonna hafta fight sooner or later. Besides, if I'd gone in their pack I'd need to do stuff I couldn't live with. I'd sooner give them half my food, and I ain't gonna do that."

"I still think you're crazy. Let's go in."

We wandered back to our cages and went inside, pretty soon a guard came by and locked us down. Dakota paced in his cell, he seemed to be full of energy. I sure wasn't. I lay on the hard concrete floor to try to get some sleep, it'd been a tough day and I was exhausted, mind and body. My body relaxed but my mind wandered.

By now, Robert should've gotten home and figured out I was gone. He had time to change his clothes, feed Meatloaf, look around for me and realize I was lost. Then he'd call the dog pound, or drive right over. He'd be here soon, I'm sure.

The barking and whining settled down, things got calmer in the cages. I rolled on my back, stuck four feet in the air and stared at the ceiling. The screws shut down some of the lights and it seemed more like dusk in the building. I thought about the pack in my little neighborhood. I wondered what Meatloaf was doing, what he was thinking. I should have talked to him before I left. Maybe he'll go to the nightly meeting and talk to the dogs, run around before they come get me.

I missed my friends and the camaraderie, I wondered if they'd ever forgive me for being an idiot about the coyotes. What was I thinking? Coyotes are wild, they're gonna do what coyotes do. I could live with being stupid, I didn't know if I could live without my friends. I shouldn't have been so independent. I need human help and dog companionship, I can't do it alone.

One dog I didn't miss was Bandit. He was probably feeling pretty cocky, probably tryin' to stealing my pooch right now. Simba will likely think he's brilliant and I'm a dumb mutt. Hah. He ran away like a scalded dog when that big coyote came in the park, leavin' her all alone to fight him off. She should realize he's a coward. But he's such a weasel, I'm sure he'll try to spin it. He'll be tellin' Simba what a loser I am.

On the other paw, she might think I'm either gone for good or going soon. I mean, our house is for sale. We're off to prison. Since I'm out of the picture, she may as well stick with him.

And Meatloaf, how's he gonna manage in this pound? He's got that limp, I know the packs will pick on him. I think he's too old to get another human. He doesn't know it yet, but he may be in here until he dies, getting by as one of the Outcast, always hungry.

It seems very late now, most of the dogs are sleeping. It looks like Robert's not gonna come get me after all. He probably figures he might as well leave me here, instead of picking me up and taking me back again when the house sells. That means tomorrow I've got to fight the Blacks and get my butt kicked. I might have a chance fighting if I had some friends in here to help me.

But I don't.

It's funny how you can lose your pals just like that. I thought Gizmo and Roxie and Winston were my buddies. We had such good times tryin' to solve Vicki's murder. And we almost did figure it out, we were so close I could smell it. If only we'd found the killer, everything would be fine right now. But instead, my life is a total bust and I'm a failure.

The guards turned the lights down even more.   It was almost dark in the pound, but inside my steel cage everything seemed totally black.   I put my chin on the floor and let out a deep sigh.   Far across the room, a new fish whimpered like a lost puppy.

I knew just how he felt.

TWENTY-EIGHT

Thud.

Meatloaf's eyes popped open when the papers-human dropped her bundle on the driveway. He lay there staring at the wall, waiting for light-time and Robert to get up and go to work. If his master knew Taser was at the pound, he'd go get him. But Robert thought his dog was out in the desert, dead. Only Meatloaf knew the truth, so it was up to him.

Last night, he lay awake a long time, using his brain like Dominga said. He lay awake until he came up with a plan.

The Animal Control people took Taser to the pound because he wasn't wearing his collar, they didn't know his name or where he lived. Meatloaf thought this was his fault. Ever since he got his own collar caught in the dog door, both their collars stayed in the drawer. He made this mess so he had to fix it. All he had to do was take Taser's collar and tag to the people at the pound. They'd call Robert to come pick him up.

Once he had his plan, he could hardly wait for Robert to leave. He nosed at his breakfast but didn't eat it. He wasn't hungry, he was too excited. Robert looked at him with concern, but gave him another hug and went off to work with his friend from the bank. Robert still didn't have his new Jeep. He probably didn't care about a car right now, he'd lost his dog.

But Meatloaf was gonna fix that.

He went to the kitchen drawer and pulled on the knob with his teeth. He sniffed both collars, then bit into the red one with Taser's tag and dragged it out.

176

Now came the hard part.

He had to get out of the house and the yard. That was a problem because he couldn't work those round door-things. He couldn't jump and flip the side yard gate latch like Gizmo. He stood there with the collar in his mouth, then went out the dog door and dropped it by the side gate. Maybe he could force it.

He pushed on the gate with his nose. It swung out, then back in. He backed up and ran at it and pushed with his paws. It swung out, then back in. He sat down and thought about the situation.

This was specism. The humans get to roam free but the dogs are locked up. We know human words but they don't know any of ours. Dominga was right.

He put it out of his mind and tried something else. Meatloaf took a walk along the fence, sniffing and examining every bit of it. He'd never tried to breakout before, so he'd never looked for a weak spot. When he got to the other side of the yard, he heard Harley roaming around in his backyard.

Harley.

Harley was an escape artist, he broke out all the time, he'd know what to do.

Meatloaf ran to the rear view-fence and barked until his neighbor showed up at the same rear corner and spoke to him.

"Whatsa racket, Jack?"

"Harley, I got to get out of here, out of the yard, can you help me?"

"You horney or somethin'?"

"I need to take Taser his collar. They took him to the pound because they didn't know where he lived."

"So what, you goin' down to the pound?"

"If I can get out of here. Can you help me?

"Lets say you gets outta the yard, what then? You gonna call a cab or take the bus?"

"I got a plan. I'm going down to the main road and wander out in the street. Some human will worry I'm gonna get hit by a car and pick me up and take me to the pound."

"Jack, that's the dumbest plan I ever heard. You gonna gets yourself killed."

Meatloaf wasn't about to be dissuaded.

"So how do you breakout? You're the expert."

"Myself, I like to dig out, so I can leave whenever I want. But these houses got too much see-ment. Best for me is wait for the cleaning-humans. They leave the door open to carry in their stuff and I slip out the front."

"We don't have cleaning-humans."

"You got anything broke? Works the same when repair-humans come."

"I can't wait that long."

"How about the pool-human?"

"We don't have a swimming pool."

"Meter-human?"

"I need to go today, Harley."

"You in a heap a trouble, Jack. Can you gets in the garage?"

"I don't know, why?"

"You gets in the garage, all you gotta do is push that button on the side of the door. That big garage door opens and you're free."

"I don't know, I don't think I can get in there, the door is shut." Meatloaf hung his head. "Maybe it's hopeless."

"Don't be getting' all negative on me, Jack. You can do this. Fact is, you needs a tool to get out. You needs a human."

More specism. "There's no human here."

"We're gonna get you one. Can you squeal?"

"Squeal? Like crying?"

"Yeah, like—Hee! Hee! Hee!"

The sound hurt Meatloaf's ears.

"Enough! Yeah, I can do that."

178

"Good. You know that Bulldog in the neighborhood?"

"Winston, yeah. He's in our pack."

"Won't be long now, he'll be walkin' his humans by the house. They're old and they don't work. Come by every day."

"And they're my tool."

"That's right. You start squealin' like you caught in a bear trap and they come open the gate to help you. Then you bolt."

"Harley, that's brilliant."

"Sure you wanna do this? It's an ugly world out there, Jack."

Meatloaf took a deep breath. He wasn't sure, but he was committed to try.

"He's my buddy. He'd do it for me."

"All right, then. Here's what we do. You go wait by the gate, I'll watch for 'em from the upstairs window. When I see 'em comin' down the street, I'll run down and bark twice."

"Thanks, Harley. How can I repay you?"

"Maybe someday you'll help me breakout. But watch your back, Jack. Most humans aren't as nice as ours."

Meatloaf ran back to the side and moved the red collar away from the gate. He sat down in the shade of the house and waited for Harley's bark, all poised and ready to slip out. He was nervous, he'd never been out on the street alone, but figured he didn't have much to lose. One way or the other, he was going to the pound.

Time passed without any warning from Harley. Meatloaf started getting tired, on a normal day he'd be asleep by now. He fought the urge to close his eyes by pacing back and forth. Soon the day warmed up and he got thirsty, so he ran inside for a drink, figuring it may be the last water he'd have until he got to see Taser. He gulped at the bowl until he heard two sharp barks from next door.

Now!

Meatloaf stuck half his body through the dog door and started crying.

"Eee Eee Eee Eee Eee!"

It sounded like someone was murdering him. Almost immediately a human was at their gate, peering through the slats.

It's Robert's dog, a female said.

"Eee Eee Eee Eee Eee!"

They fiddled with the gate latch and finally got it open.

What's wrong, puppy?

Meatloaf felt bad he had to scare the nice old couple, but he figured desperate times called for desperate measures. When they both got inside the gate to help him, he wiggled out, picked up the red collar and ran out to the street. The humans were too surprised to speak, but Winston yelled at him as he ran by.

"Hey!"

Meatloaf ignored him and kept running. He ran all the way down their street and past the grassy park. He ran past Simba's house and Spike's street. He only slowed down when he came to the exit road from the subdivision. He turned around and looked back, thankful no one was following him. He dropped Taser's collar and stood there, panting just outside the neighborhood.

The exit road curved around and went down to the main road to the city. It looked awful far away, so he thought he'd take a shortcut straight through the desert. When he felt better, he picked up the collar and trotted out through the brush, making a beeline for the main road.

Meatloaf had been in the desert before, but only on well-worn trails when hiking with Robert. This was different, there were no trails and the ground wasn't flat or forgiving underfoot. This desert land was close to the mountains, so there were steep-sided gullys and rocky areas everywhere. He thought he was saving time and trouble, but the terrain turned out to be tougher than it looked.

Meatloaf stopped to make sure he was still heading straight toward the main road. The sun baked his black coat so much he thought he better cool off under a silver Brittlebrush bush. He lay there panting, unmindful of the sharp granite floor jabbing him in the belly. He was determined to save his friend, so he put minor pains out of his mind.

Soon a swarm of tiny sand flies soon discovered him, and they were a major pain. The buzzing around his eyes forced him to his feet and on his way. He stepped down in a narrow wash and followed it for a long while, happy the sand felt soft and cool to his feet. Eventually the sides of the wash soon got steep, too steep to get out, so he started to backtrack.

The rattling stopped him.

It was either the rattling or his innate dog sense that brought him to a halt. He must have disturbed the rattler's slumber as it lay tucked under a rock outcrop, hiding from the sun on the soft sand of the wash.

Meatloaf froze. He dared not walk past this menace again.

The snake had his tail stuck out from under the rock, rattling a warning. It was a Diamondback rattler and most of its five-foot length was out of sight, but Meatloaf could see its head and serpent tongue testing the air under the outcrop. That was more than enough for Meatloaf.

He moved two steps further away from the rattler. The wash sides narrowed even more, but he thought he could get out there. As he climbed up the rocky sides, loose pieces of granite gave way as Meatloaf slid down and landed in a noisy pile. He leaped to his feet and got as far away as possible from the rattlesnake.

Now the rattler wound its speckled body all the way out from under its rock and raised its head, tongue searching for the hostile heat source. Meatloaf jammed himself against the wall and let loose a little whimper. He was three dog-lengths from the disturbed Diamondback, but somehow he knew the snake could bridge that gap in one strike.

He stood very still.

The snake's head swayed.

The sun beat down on them both.

181

Then the sand flies arrived, buzzing Meatloaf's ears and bombarding his eyes. He shook his head slightly—then froze as the snake looked right at him.

I am a rabbit, Meatloaf thought.

I am a stone rabbit.

The sand flies buzzed the rabbit's head.

The rabbit didn't move a whisker.

Slowly, the snake lowered his head and uncurled his body. He moved sideways, sliding back under his rock.

Meatloaf didn't wait a moment longer. He lunged at the side of the wash, bouncing off one side and then the other and scrambling over the top. Then he ran.

The creosote raked his coat as he dodged and weaved through the brush, putting maximum distance between him and the rattlesnake. He stopped close to the main road, panting and wheezing like a scared Black Labrador.

Finally, he was safe at the side of the highway.

TWENTY-NINE

Whimpering is one thing, but when some Dalmatian near my cage howled later on it woke me up. I stared at the ceiling, thinkin' it was somewhere in the middle of the dark-time. My stomach was growling because now I was starvin'. I scrunched up on the floor so my belly wouldn't hurt so bad. Some mutts were snorin' and some were talkin' in their sleep, so I looked over at my neighbor to see if he was up. It was tough to tell, all I could see was his round form on the floor.

"Hey Dakota, you awake?"

He grunted.

"I could probably eat some of that pound swill now."

"Hmm. Too late, I ate it all. Go back to sleep."

"I'm too hungry to sleep."

"I tried to tell you," he said.

"If I only had a big bowl of canned dog-food. I love that smell when they open the can. I start droolin' as soon as I hear the poof."

Dakota yawned. "My favorite thing is leftover gravy poured right over my dry food. Yum."

"We don't get many leftovers," I said, "but I usually get a mini hamburger if there's extra meat when they barbeque."

"I love hamburgers. Sometimes when we're working I get a burger for lunch, with cheese if I'm lucky. And those french fries."

"So tell me, what's the best meal you ever had?"

"Lemme think," he said. "Probably day after last Christmas. Jimmy—that's my human—gave me a bunch of left-over chicken enchiladas. He was drinking and not thinking too good. I ate the

183

whole thing. It was wonderful, but the green chilies gave me diarrhea for a week."

"Sounds great."

"What about you?"

I knew already, I'd been thinking about it. "Thanksgiving Day. We get a special plate with turkey and stuffing, mashed potatoes and gravy, just for us. It's awesome."

Or it would be, if I was home for Thanksgiving this year.

"One time I had a huge T-bone steak," Dakota said. "Jimmy barbequed it for me special, we ate out on the patio one night. I ate the whole thing, and then I ate the bone. The weather was just right, not too cold or hot. It would have been the perfect meal, except for the smell."

"Why, did he burn the steak?"

"No, it was the yard. The stinking yard. He'd fertilized it that day. The guy is really good, he has a green thumb, but he should have waited to put that manure down."

I sat up when he said green thumb. I jumped to my feet at the word manure.

"Did you say manure?"

"Yeah, I know. Cow poop. Didn't mean to ruin your food fantasy."

"No, no. Listen, tell me about manure."

"What's to tell? It's a great fertilizer, nitrogen rich. Greens your yard right up. But that smell."

"What about greening up your trees?"

"No, dog. You never put it on your plants or trees, it's too hot. The nitrogen will burn 'em, kill 'em dead."

I'm standing right at his cage bars now. "So a guy who knew what he was doing would never put manure on his trees?"

"No way."

"Especially a guy with a green thumb?"

"Black thumb, maybe."

Of course. Now I knew.

We were so close I could smell it.

I even said it to myself. How could I have been so stupid.

There was only one answer for what happened to the tree in Vicki's back yard. I knew who killed her and I could prove it. But stuck in the pound, I couldn't do a thing about it.

Somehow, I had to get out of there.

THIRTY

The road to Phoenix had more traffic then Meatloaf had ever seen. Huge construction and delivery trucks blasted by his spot at the side of the road. Meatloaf stood his ground, trying to look lost and pathetic.

Nobody seemed to care.

He thought maybe if he got on the road itself, people would stop. So Meatloaf stepped onto the roadway.

HONNNNNNK!

He jumped off the road as a cement truck blew by with an obnoxious air horn blaring. He looked to either side, it seemed the cars were moving too fast to walk on the road. This was going to be harder than he thought. He decided to put the collar down and sit on the side of the street, maybe the humans driving by would think he was trying to cross over. That should make them nervous, too. He sat there a while, hoping the right person would drive by and rescue him. The problem was, there seemed to be a lot of business trucks on this road. He didn't think they would stop for him, but he didn't want to move to a different street.

Meatloaf was panting hard, wishing it wasn't so hot in the day-light when an older model car stopped on the shoulder of the road, just ahead of him. The driver walked back and looked at him. It was a male-human about as old as Robert, he seemed nice enough when he spoke.

Are you lost?

No, I live here, genius. Take me to the pound.

The human stuck out the back of his hand, slowly.

You friendly, boy?

Meatloaf sniffed the hand, politely. Toothpaste. Cigarettes. McDonald's egg McMuffin.

You look friendly.

I'm a Labrador, don't you know anything? Friendly is our job.

Come on, boy.

The human walked back to his car, looking back to see if Meatloaf was following. He reached inside and retrieved a used soda cup and a bottle of water. He poured all of the water in the cup and held it for Meatloaf to drink. He slurped all he could reach until his muzzle stuck too far in to get any more. The cup smelled like a soda his Fresno human used to drink, mountain something.

Then Meatloaf remembered the collar. He ran back and picked it up and brought it to the car. He was worried his rescuer would see the address or phone number on the tag and take him directly home. It was the one flaw in his plan, a problem he hadn't been able to solve.

He needn't have worried, the human leaned down to look at the tag and then opened the door. He didn't seem interested in it at all, he just threw the collar on the seat.

Hop in, Killer.

Killer?

Meatloaf ignored the slight and jumped in the back seat next to Taser's collar. The human got in front and they drove down the main road toward Phoenix. Meatloaf watched the traffic from the rear window. So far, he thought, his plan was working perfectly.

Meatloaf sniffed the car for clues about his rescue-human. The first thing he noticed was the human's breath, which was interesting to a dog but probably not to other humans. Next he smelled a strong odor of carpet glue and fibers, many different kinds. Maybe the guy was a carpet construction worker. He'd seen them come and put in new carpet at the last human's house. But no, this guy had nicer clothes, he looked like a human who talked for a living.

He figured the guy was probably a carpet-talker, because there had to be pieces of carpet in the trunk, the smell was too strong to be

187

anywhere but in the car with them. He kept sniffing. The human had a mate, too. There was perfume in the air, but only one kind, not different scents from different females. Personally, he hated perfume, it overpowered his nose.

He knew something else about her, he could tell she was a drinker like his last female. He picked up sweat on the front passenger seat, Meatloaf could tell the perfume mixed with sweat from too-many days without a bath. The sweat was laced with alcohol and the odor of juniper berries.

There was a pup with them, too. He sniffed out dirty socks, milk chocolate, grease from a bicycle chain and pup urine. He figured that had to be a male. Too bad, little males were a pain in the butt. Little females were fine, they just hugged you and talked nice to you. Some little males thought dogs were small horses or punching bags.

They'd been driving for a while and now the neighborhoods looked different. Meatloaf wasn't sure where the pound was, but he thought they must be close to it by now. They were off the freeway and somewhere in a residential neighborhood in the Phoenix town, that's all he knew for sure. The houses were smaller and older than Robert's, but nice looking. When they stopped at one of the houses, Meatloaf noticed the paint was peeling and the yard was full of weeds. This house seemed to be the worst-kept one on the street.

His human pulled in the driveway and opened the rear car door.

Come on, boy.

He motioned toward the house.

Meatloaf knew this wasn't the pound, but he figured the guy had to stop here first to use the bathroom, so he obeyed. He put the collar in his mouth and jumped out. The human bent down and put his hand on it.

I'll take it.

Meatloaf let go reluctantly and watched the guy put Taser's collar in his front pocket. He sat down in protest. This was not part of the plan, this guy shouldn't keep his collar.

188

Come on, Killer.

The carpet-talker walked to the side-yard gate. Meatloaf followed, thinking maybe he should have picked a different rescue-human. He mumbled to himself.

Just give me my collar back, buddy, and I'm out of here.

Meatloaf followed him in the back yard, where he watched the human put Taser's collar in the garbage can.

Hey, hold on, there.

What the hell is that?

They both turned to see a woman on the patio, Meatloaf recognized her smell as the mate. She was wearing what looked like a tent or a baggy sheet. Meatloaf hadn't seen a dress this big before, but it could have been a dress.

What'd you bring home now?

It's a dog.

I can see that, idiot. What's it doing here?

I picked him up in Scottsdale, somebody abandoned him. I figured we could use a good watch dog.

Wait a minute, fella. You got the wrong pooch. I don't do night work.

She looked Meatloaf over.

He looks clean. Well-kept. Maybe there's a reward out for him.

This dog? No way. His owner didn't take care of him so he ran off. He limps, the owner didn't even fix him.

That's great, Fred. What good is a watchdog that limps?

Hey, I'm still plenty dangerous, even with my limp.

He'll bark. Burglars won't know he's crippled.

She walked out in the back yard and squinted.

What kind of dog is it?

He's a Rottweiler.

I'm a Labrador, genius, and I'm not gonna be you're watchdog. Now give me back my collar.

He looks kinda stupid.

189

All dogs are stupid. But we need a watchdog, two robberies in one month, that's crazy.

She bent down and called to Meatloaf.

Come here, puppy.

Meatloaf didn't move. He didn't answer to humans who insulted him.

She stood up and put her hands on her hips.

See, he is stupid. What's his name?

Killer.

She tried again.

Come here, Killer.

Meatloaf backed up two steps and sat down again. This was not working out like he planned.

Damn dog doesn't like me. What good is he?

He'll warm up to you.

What if he bites little Freddie, then what're you gonna do then?

He'll love Junior.

He touches my Freddie, I swear I'll shoot him.

Honey, you worry too much. Come on, let's eat some lunch.

He turned to Meatloaf.

Killer, Stay!

Stay? Stay this, fella.

They went in the house and left Meatloaf alone. He walked further out and sat in the dirt under a drooping Eucalyptus tree. The yard looked like it had grass once, but it was mostly dead now, only a few dead patches with healthy weeds remained. He glanced around at this strange new environment. It didn't seem dog friendly at all. No chew toys. No food. No—

Hey, where's my water!

Meatloaf sighed. He should have thought of a different plan.

THIRTY-ONE

The noise started early in the joint, but I'd been awake awhile, thinking about the inevitable fight today. I stretched one rear-leg out straight behind me, then the other, then walked around to warm up. My shoulder wound didn't feel too bad, so I yanked the bandage off so I wouldn't look weak.

When first meal arrived I ate it all, it tasted pretty good to me now, I was starved. I noticed Dakota left half in his bowl, but I didn't say anything, I didn't want to be critical of my new friend. I asked him about his human to change the subject.

"Your Jimmy, you think he'll be out soon?"

"Dunno. Everytime it gets longer. I wish he'd give up the drinking."

That reminded me I was thirsty, I went over to the water and drank some down. Amazing. Even the water in this place stank. Sometimes I wished my nose wasn't so good.

I stood there thinking about the right way to handle Digger. Dakota saw me looking out into the pound.

"So Taser. You gonna fight the big guy today?"

"Doesn't look like I have much choice."

"I thought you said he was afraid to fight."

"No. I said he was afraid to get hurt."

Dakota couldn't see the difference.

"Aggression," I said. "He'll hesitate at a critical moment. It's his weak spot."

"It's not too late, you could tell them you'd join."

I didn't answer, I just paced in my cage and checked things out. Most of the other mutts were standing around, waiting for the screws

191

to spring them for yard-time. I was ready to go too, I was psyched to fight. When the doors started opening, me and Dakota were some of the first dogs out. We walked down the hall to the yard, catching the look of some of the Black pack. Apparently the word was out.

Dakota nudged me as we walked.

"You see that?" he asked.

"The evil eye. Yeah, I saw it." I glanced around. "How many Blacks they got in here?"

Dakota snorted. "What difference does it make, you gonna fight them all? Anything over two is your death sentence."

I didn't say anything, but I only planned to fight Digger. If I could handle Digger, the rest wouldn't mess with me.

I hoped.

We did our business and then took our place along the wall. Dogs filed in slowly. Some ran around once they were inside, some just sat down. Most were typical mixed-breed mutts that their humans let run loose or got lost. The Outcast dogs stayed away from the ruling pack-dogs, they wandered around in the middle while the packs lined-up on opposite sides of the yard. Only the crazy dogs barked, oblivious of their environment.

Digger wasn't in yet but some of his Black Pack was. They stared at me as they came in. I looked away and ignored them.

I noticed Paco, head of the Browns, looking me over. True to his group, Paco's coat was brown except for white paws, neck and muzzle. One ear tip was chewed cleanly off. Because his ears stood straight up, the difference made him look lopsided. Paco seemed average size for a Bull Terrier, but the breed was intimidating even at medium size. Bull Terriers were muscular, pumped-up. They looked overinflated, like a hundred-pound dog in a fifty-pound skin. They were a tough-looking bunch in my mind.

Paco stared at me a while, then he leaned down and said something to a wiry Chihuahua at his side. The little pooch ran toward the spot where we were sitting.

Dakota saw him coming.

"Oh, boy, here we go. Now you've pissed off the other pack. What is it about you, Taze?"

The Chihuahua ran right up to me. "Mister Paco would like to have a word with you."

I looked at Dakota. At least the L.A. transplant had manners. "Tell your boss I'll be right over."

I sat and watched the toy dog run off with my answer.

"Whadda ya think, Dakota? He doesn't sound crazy to me."

"Watch yourself, he can be polite one moment and psycho the next. He'll turn on you. Call him Mister Paco, everyone else does."

I got up and trotted over, not too fast, not too slow. Respectful but not subservient. I stopped in front of him, just out of biting distance. Paco was flanked by Browns, most of them looked like mixed breeds, ex-street dogs. This pack seemed more dangerous to me than the Blacks, especially Paco.

Paco's scars were even worse close up. He looked like he'd been sewn up by a drunk, but somehow it added to his macho. He carried the air of a confident alpha, like he'd come-up from the bottom of a rough neighborhood.

I waited for him to speak first. I didn't have to wait long.

"I hear you're fightin' Digger today."

I didn't say anything. I figured every dog in the joint must know by now.

"You some bad-ass pooch or just stupid?"

I noticed Digger walking into the yard. "I guess we'll find out."

Paco noticed Digger come in, too. Then he looked me over, close up. "They say you're crazy."

"Funny, that's what they say about you."

He chuckled. "This place will do that to you."

"You seem to be doin' all right. You got half the turf, half the power, half the food."

"Takes a lot of chow to run a pack like ours. We gotta defend ourselves from the Blacks."

I'd heard that before. "That's the excuse Digger uses to take food. Why don't you guys just chill out and enjoy our weather."

"A comedian, too. I'm impressed."

"You're from LA. You got lots of comedians over there, you should be used to it."

Apparently he didn't appreciate all my humor. His mood darkened.

"Careful, mutt. Don't forget you're on your own in here. You don't want to piss-off the whole pound."

He was right, of course. I was just tryin' to figure out what he wanted with me.

"I meant no disrespect, Mr. Paco."

He softened.

"None taken."

I thought I'd just ask him. "I'm curious about our meeting. Why the questions?"

"I wanna know a little more about you. You from Arizona?"

"Born and raised."

"You ever been in the pound? You seem to know the lay of the land."

"I was here when there were no packs. All you had to deal with was the guards hassling you."

"See, I protect my boys from the screws. Nothin' like bite on the ass to straighten out a two-leg."

He was quiet a while. I waited until he spoke again.

"How old are you, kid?"

I thought that was a funny question, but I answered him. "I'm five."

"You ever had another two-leg?"

"Couple others."

He looked at my head. "Your ears. They seem big for your breed. That a mix somewhere back in your line?"

"Blue Tic Hound." I was losin' patience. "You writing a book?"

This time he chuckled, then said, "I see a lot of dogs come through here, none act like you. They come in scared, they don't make trouble."

"I just want to be left alone."

"Now, I respect that. But you're makin' it tough for us to keep control. Dogs start thinkin' they don't hafta do what we say, pretty soon discipline breaks down. They gang-up, stop giving us their food. It's only a thin brown line."

I knew now what the problem was. It wasn't looking good for me, no way could I fight both groups. I glanced over at Digger. It looked like he wanted to settle our differences.

"What would you have me do, Mister Paco? I'm already fighting with Digger over this."

He raised a paw. "Please, just call me Paco."

"Paco. I can't live under any dog's toe. Not after what I've been through in my life."

He seemed to consider that.

"Excuse me one moment," he said.

He bent over and conversed with the Chihuahua at his side. The tiny mutt appeared to be his consigliore. After the discussion, he scampered across the floor of the yard to Digger and talked to him. Digger said something to his companion dogs and walked over alone.

That's great, I thought. Now there's two of them.

Paco sent away his own Brown bodyguards. When Digger arrived, it was just the two pack heads with me and the Chihuahua.

Paco spoke first to Digger.

"Thank you for coming. I called this meeting so we might resolve our problem with Taser here."

"Yeah? Why should we treat him different?"

"He is different."

"You're crazy. We can't have the new fish disrespect us."

"Taser is a special case. I feel we should offer him our respect."

Digger snorted. "Why? He offers me none. The punk insults me in front of my mutts."

Paco looked at me. "Is that true?"

I shrugged.

"No matter," Paco said, "It's my feeling we should grant him a pardon. An exemption from joining the packs or the Outcasts."

"Never. He's not leavin' this yard in one piece."

Paco stood up. "My friend, I think a fight would be a mistake. Even if you won."

I couldn't understand why Paco was stickin' up for me. Especially since he complained about my rockin' the boat.

Digger looked insulted. "Whadda you mean, if I win. I'm gonna eat this dog for lunch. No punk disses me on my turf."

"We risk losing respect from the Outcasts. No respect, no control. We can't afford that to satisfy your ego."

"They won't respect me if this insult goes unpunished."

"Not to their hero. If I'm right, we lose even if you win."

Digger looked in my direction. "Him? A hero? Gimme a break. Just because you refuse my offer doesn't make you a hero."

"Digger, shut up and listen. We've never talked about this before, I'm not sure what you know." Paco stood up. "When I first came to this pound, they used to tell stories about the meanest Pit Bull there ever was. A dog that lived to kill."

I caught his glance.

Digger spoke up impatiently. "Yeah, yeah. I know all about this Zeus. What's the point?"

"If you know about Zeus, you know about Chili. They still talk about that day. This Chili was tougher than anyone in the pound. The only dog with the guts to attack Zeus to save his friend. The only dog savage enough to rip the guts from a Pit Bull's loins."

He looked around the pound, then he continued.

"He was just an average mutt. He was black, but his color didn't make the difference. He was only a Labrador, but his breed didn't make the difference. The difference was his heart."

Paco turned to me. "I spoke to Major, the old Shepard, about this dog many times. He said Chili was a male Black Lab with big ears. He would be your age now."

Now they all looked at me.

Paco asked. "Your last two-leg, what did he call you?"

I hesitated, then told them the truth. "My name then was Chili."

Digger backed up a step. Paco nodded with respect. Nobody said anything for a moment, then the consigliore spoke.

"I propose a truce for Taser. The Blacks and the Browns will leave him alone and he will leave us alone. He will get all his food portion with no quarrel from us." The Chihuahua looked at both pack heads. "Agreed?"

"Agreed," said Paco.

Digger spoke through clenched teeth.

"Agreed."

I wasn't quite sure what to say, but I felt I'd gotten a reprieve. Frankly, I was grateful.

"Thank you, both." I turned to the head of the Browns. "Paco, I need to know, you said you knew Major. What happened to him, did he die in here."

"No. He's alive. He was rescued by an old couple that wanted a calm dog, they took him to their home in Prescott. He was in good health when he left here."

Great. Major finally made it to the cool country.

I excused myself, then jogged back over next to Dakota. He was waiting in the same spot, having seen the whole thing. He glanced at the pack leaders, then spoke quietly.

"What the heck was that?" he asked.

I was still surprised. "A reprieve."

"A reprieve? What for?"

197

I thought about something important I'd almost forgotten.

"It's my last chance to catch a killer."

Dakota just stared.

THIRTY-TWO

Meatloaf was so engrossed in chewing that he didn't notice the carpet-talker approaching. He heard the guy yelling first.

NO! Bad dog. That's garbage!

Fred picked up Taser's red collar and the trash from the tipped-over garbage can and put it back in the righted can.

Bad dog!

Meatloaf looked at him with a mixture of disdain and defiance.

Yeah, yeah. I hear ya.

Then the carpet-talker had a long talk with him, but Meatloaf tuned him out and didn't hear a word. He was thinking what Taser would do in this predicament. He'd already checked the soft fence line, he knew he could dig out, but he'd have to wait for night-time because it would take a while. He didn't want to be discovered digging. Then he heard the word 'Freddie' .

He looked at the house as a small boy barreled out the back door, yelling and screaming something. The pup-human made a beeline for him and grabbed him tight around the neck. He squeezed until Meatloaf's head bent sideways.

My own dog! Oh Boy!

No Freddie, Killer is our new watchdog. But you can play with him.

Freddie didn't seem to understand.

My own dog! Finally I have my own dog!

He held Meatloaf tight and pulled him up on his feet.

Now play gentle, Freddie. Remember what happened to your rabbit.

Freddie let loose and ran around the yard, waving his arms up and down like a bird and yelling with joy. Meatloaf watched in amazement, wondering if they might have any mushrooms growing in this yard he could give the kid.

Just then little Freddie tripped on his own feet and fell face first. He got up crying and swinging his fists. The female-human ran out of the house and tried to comfort him.

Calm down, Freddie. You're all right.

She brushed the dirt off the front of his food-stained t-shirt.

Come inside and I'll give you some ice cream and chocolate sauce.

Freddie let himself be led inside, sniffling and punching at the invisible enemy who'd knocked him down. Meatloaf looked at the male carpet-talker. He hadn't moved to help during the whole disaster, he stood there like this was a normal day.

Then he looked down at Meatloaf.

I'm going back to work, Killer. If you protect the house from burglars, I'll bring you some dinner.

That's not how it works, pal. Dinner comes first.

Meatloaf watched him leave and went back under the shade of his tree. This human was a catbrain. He still had no water dish, but he'd gotten some water by licking the leaking backyard hose. He was hungry now, so he searched the ground under the Eucalyptus tree for pods or anything he could eat. There weren't any seed pods, but he found a grape popsicle stick that he chewed up. Then he located something on the ground he couldn't identify, but it stunk real bad and was kinda crunchy, so he ate that, too. He thought it might have been alive once, but not recently. He figured if it wasn't any good, no problem, he could always throw it up later.

He probably should have eaten all his food from first meal, but he was too excited about breaking out and getting on the road. Now all he could do was wait. Meatloaf put his head down and slept the best he could in the heat. He dreamed he was back in Fresno, eating garbage out of the tipped-over can, then throwing it up.

Bingo.

Meatloaf woke from his dream, realizing it was the solution to his problem.

He went back to the garbage can and pushed it over, the lid rolled away and garbage spilled out on the ground. Meatloaf sniffed around until he located Taser's collar. He picked it up and went back under the tree. It was hard not to take the wrapper from the hamburger or the empty french-fry box, but he resisted.

Just then little Freddie burst out back, wired even further after his chocolate sundae. Freddie went to the side of the house and retrieved a battered bicycle with bent training wheels. He hopped on and started making laps around the yard, trailing little clouds of dust behind him.

On his third loop around he aimed his bike at Meatloaf reclining under his tree. When a collision seemed inevitable, Meatloaf jumped gracefully out of the way. Freddie went by but turned around for another pass.

This time he aimed right at his new pet, so Meatloaf started trotting away with Freddie hot on his tail. Pretty soon they were both making laps around the yard, an irritated black dog followed by a determined problem child.

Freddie!

The female human screamed from the patio at her errant son.

Don't bother that stupid dog, he might bite you. What if he has rabies? I swear, sometimes…

She mumbled to herself as she walked back in the house. Freddie got off his bicycle and sat down in the dirt.

Meatloaf watched warily from his cool spot in the shade. He wished he'd started digging out already. This kid was trouble and he couldn't wait to get out of here. Besides, he was concerned something might happen to Taser in the pound, there wasn't a lot of time to waste.

Freddie picked up some small stones from the yard and started tossing them in Meatloaf's direction. They fell short of target, but the insult didn't go unnoticed. Normally when threatened, Meatloaf would stand close to his master for protection, but now he had no one to help him.

OK, kid, you're starting to make me mad.

Freddie must have thought he'd stumbled on a good idea by throwing stones, he seemed to have the upper hand in this game. He searched the yard for larger rocks, walking closer to Meatloaf with each throw. When he finally connected with a rock to the rear, Meatloaf jumped and ran to the other side of the yard.

Freddie squealed with his new-found power. He advanced on his four-legged prey until he had him backed into a corner.

When Meatloaf felt the second rock hit, he just reacted. He charged forward and knocked Freddie off his feet. But this time he didn't run away. He circled Freddie, and when the kid got up on two feet, Meatloaf grabbed him by the seat of his dusty Levis and dragged him around the yard backwards, tugging and jerking.

Freddie howled and swatted at him but couldn't reach him. Meatloaf yanked the little screamer around until his mother ran into the yard and started screaming herself. Meatloaf growled like a rabid dog while he pulled, finally little Freddie fell and his crying escalated. The female human scooped up her son and ran in the house, leaving Meatloaf panting in the yard, proud of his response to the personal attack.

He looked up when the female returned muttering and carrying a long black stick. She struggled to put it to her shoulder and aimed at him. The best she could do was get it pointed in his general direction. Meatloaf sat watching, head cocked to one side, curious about what was happening. He felt no danger, only fascination with this strange female.

She fumbled with the black object for a while but it only seemed to make her madder. Finally she lowered the stick and screeched at him.

I'll fix you, you stupid mutt! I'm calling the dogcatcher. You're going to the dog pound!

The human stumbled back in the house and slammed the door and locked it. Meatloaf walked back to his tree and stretched out in the shade. He exhaled a long, slow breath.

Oh no, lady. Anything but that.

THIRTY-THREE

All of a sudden the barking got louder. That meant there was a fight in the yard or a new inmate had arrived.

The noise interrupted my afternoon nap, so I cracked one eye and scoped the hallway from my spot on the floor. It looked like a Labrador comin' in. I don't get excited about the fish anymore, but this black dog limped in a strangely familiar way. All of a sudden my tail started thumpin' the floor.

What the heck?

I jumped to my feet and called out. "Meatloaf?"

My partner stopped in his tracks right in front of my cage and looked at me with wide eyes. He seemed tired and his coat was full of burrs and brown dust, but it was definitely Meatloaf.

"Taser! I gotta talk to you."

"What're you—"

Before I could finish, the guard yanked on his leash and half-drug him to his new home across the building. I couldn't believe my colorblind eyes. The last dog I expected to run into at the pound was Meatloaf.

"Who's that?" asked Dakota.

I was still stunned. "My... My partner. The dog I was telling you about, the mutt I live with in Scottsdale. I can't figure out why he's here."

"Maybe he went looking for you and got picked up by the same guy."

I didn't think so, Meat wasn't the adventuresome kind. I was mystified by the whole event.

"Hey Dakota. Pass it along to Meatloaf. Get word to him we can talk soon, at the next yard time."

"Right."

Dakota talked to the dog next to him and the message spread across the pound, cage to cage, Outcast to Outcast. They all knew who I was, the word had gotten out. Except now they called me Chili instead of Taser.

I waited impatiently for yard time so we could talk. The only thing I could think of was that Robert brought Meatloaf to the pound. Maybe I had made him mad by breaking out of the backyard.

When the guards finally opened our doors, I jogged out to the yard. Meatloaf was already there, standing in the middle.

"Dawg, am I glad to see you."

I could see that by his tail. Mine was keepin' time with his, we looked like a couple of puppies at mealtime. I gave his neck a playful bite. "What's the story? How come you're here? Robert dump you off already?"

"I came to rescue you, dawg. I worried it was my fault you ended up here, 'cause you don't have a collar and tag."

I didn't know what to say, I was afraid we were in a real mess. Now we were both stuck in the pound.

I asked him. "Robert know we're here?"

"Nah, he thinks you're lost and probably dead from the heat. We went looking for you in the desert behind the park. Robert found your blood on the ground and then I found that dead coyote. Amazing."

He nosed my shoulder wound.

"That smells painful."

The wound wasn't my concern at the moment, it was getting out of here. "Robert thinks I'm gone?"

"Gone for good. But I talked to Dominga—"

"You talked to Dominga?" I couldn't believe it, it was so unlike my shy friend.

205

"She said you killed the coyote that got Buffy. Then she said the Animal Control humans took you to the city."

"So how'd you get here?"

He told me the story of his breakout, the carpet-human rescue and the Animal Control truck picking him up. I was amazed he had it in him, but getting in the pound was only half the solution.

"Partner, it's great to see you, but now what? We can't get out of here, we're both mounted."

Meatloaf didn't seem concerned at all, he was too relaxed about the whole situation. I thought he musta found some California mushrooms in that backyard.

He looked around the room. "I need a roach."

Just then Dakota walked up. I introduced him and told him Meatloaf's incredible tale of escape.

"Awesome. You guys are amazing."

"I need a roach," Meatloaf said to him. "Can you help? A big sewer roach, preferably."

I didn't have a clue why he wanted a sewer roach, but I wasn't going to stand in his way. "Dakota, whadda you think?"

"Ahh, sure. Let me get with some of the dogs."

He trotted over to a couple Outcasts and talked to them. One of them, a wiry Australian Shepherd, helped by spreading the word. Pretty soon a cry went out in the air.

"Chili needs a roach!"

"Chili needs a roach!"

Dogs scurried all around the exercise yard, searching in corners and nooks for a roach. I watched in amazement. The Blacks and the Browns looked unsettled by all the Outcast activity. For now, the Outcasts had the upper hand just by their superior numbers. They kept calling out.

"Chili needs a roach!"

"Chili needs a roach!"

Someone yelled back. "Live or dead?"

206

Meatloaf looked at me and cocked his head.

"Chili? What's that about?"

I shrugged. "I'll tell you later."

The Australian Shepherd ran up to us with the question.

"Live or dead, Chili?"

I turned to Meatloaf for the answer.

"Either way," he said. "Dead would be best."

"Dead!" the Shepherd called out.

"Dead roach, coming over!"

Some street mutt over in the corner batted a small object with his paw and spun it out on the floor. The Outcasts kept flipping and batting it along, it looked like a miniature hockey puck on its way over to us. In no time at all it landed in front of Meatloaf, six tiny legs pointed straight at the sky. He whacked it once with his paw to make sure it was dead, then sniffed it. I waited to see what would happen next.

Meatloaf grabbed it with his mouth, threw his head back and swallowed it.

"Eeewwwwwwwwww!"

Everyone groaned in disgust. Not even a starving mutt would touch a sewer roach. I didn't seem to go down well with my partner either, he acted like he was gonna throw up. Meatloaf staggered around the floor while everybody got out of his way. When he started to retch everyone backed up further.

The roach came up first, then the pound food he'd eaten, then some lumpy mystery stuff I didn't want to know anything about. Meatloaf seemed happy with the result. He looked closely at the pile on the floor, then delicately pawed a shiny metal object away out of the mess.

I walked closer to look. It was the identification tag from my collar.

"I chewed your tag off and swallowed it before they came to get me. Ruined the collar, though."

"Clever, partner."

Dakota knew what it meant. "If you're here as a stray, that's your ticket out. They'll call your master to pick you up."

"But what about Meatloaf?" I asked. "We don't want to leave him here while I get out." The pooch had sacrificed enough for me.

We looked at each other, thinking. But Dakota figured out the solution.

"You both stand over the tag. The screws won't know which one of you threw it up."

He called out to the Outcasts. "We need a guard over here!"

All the OC dogs started barking and running around us like a riot had broken out. Pretty soon a couple guards wandered over to see what the commotion was. One of them was the heavy guy who opened the cages every morning, he was one of the nicer ones.

Hey, hey, calm down. What's the problem here?

Geez, look at that mess, Benny. I ain't cleanin' that up.

I got the last puke pile, you lightweight. It's your turn.

The fat guard looked closer at the floor.

What the hell? That his tag? Damn dog ate his own tag.

Now they both looked close.

Looks like it to me. But which dog?

Meatloaf and I stood together while Dakota backed out of the way. The guards looked at me, then they looked at Meatloaf, then they looked back at me. Finally the fat guard said—

The black one.

Don't be a smart ass. Go get the shovel and bring me some gloves, I'll call this phone number. We'll let the owner choose his own Labrador.

THIRTY-FOUR

For the second time in my life, Robert came and rescued me from the pound. I don't know which time I was happier.

He put me and Meatloaf in Judy's Volvo and we stopped at Petworld on the way home for new collars and leashes. We got matching sets. From what Robert said, mine was black and Meatloaf's was green. Robert clipped my tag to the new collar right away; I think he was worried I might get lost again. I'm not sure he knew what I'd been up to, but he wasn't mad. He treated me like a long-lost dog.

When we got home Judy was there, she even gave us a bone for a welcome home treat, then we got a big bowl of dog food. Robert put some cream on my shoulder wound and it felt a little better. This was nice, but I was more concerned about catchin' the killer than getting things back to normal.

While Robert and Judy ate some dinner, I talked to Meatloaf about what had happened in the neighborhood since I ran away.

"Not much," he said. "Except Harley said that night it rained, he saw that guy behind our house same as you did.

"I knew it. That proves it wasn't the Boulder Bandit."

"That's true. Unless it was another burglar or somethin'."

"What'd the pack have to say?"

"Let's see. They were worried about you dying out in the desert. Gizmo thought it was cool you went out to kill that coyote, but Winston thought you might have committed suicide, and Roxie said her male couldn't have killed Vicki."

"Whoa, what's this? Roxie's male what?"

"Oh, I forgot to tell you. Harley said Roxie's master was one of the males in the neighborhood mounting Vicki. Harley thinks he was mad for getting dropped for Bandit's male."

The news hit me like a large can of Skippy. "Whoa. So now we got two Vicki mount-ers?"

"Maybe three, with Robert. Makes you wonder, how'd she have time for housework?"

"You sure about this?"

"Harley saw them doing it from his upstairs window."

"But did he see Robert over there?"

Meatloaf looked tired, he lay down on the floor and sighed. "He didn't say anything about seeing Robert. But if he went over early in the morning, Harley wouldn't have seen him anyway."

It didn't matter, it didn't change my theory about the murder. I needed to talk to our pack, but it didn't look like Robert was going to take us to the park tonight. It was nearly dark out. I stood by the door and whined like my bladder was about to explode.

Henggggg. Hengggggggg. Hengggggggg.

Robert didn't make a move from his chair.

No park. You guys had enough excitement today.

I turned to Meatloaf for help.

"Partner, we need to get out so I can talk to the guys."

Meatloaf was glued to the tile, he didn't even raise his head. "Give it a rest, dawg. The pack will be there tomorrow."

Henggggg. Hengggggggg.

Hush.

I started pacing. I didn't want to wait until tomorrow. I knew who killed Vicki and I had to prove it, if not to the world, to myself. I didn't understand why no one seemed to care as much as me. Maybe we weren't moving afterall. I went to the front window to check, but the flipper sign was still up. It looked like nothing had changed since I'd been gone.

"Meat. Get up. We've got to get the guys help."

"What's the rush?"

"Is tomorrow a shiny shoe day or a rubber shoe day?"

"What's it matter?"

"We need to get in Nelly's backyard. We can't do that if the humans in the neighborhood are home. We need 'em off at work."

Now he raised his head. "You want to break out of our house again? Then break into Nelly's house? You're crazy, I'm not helping you anymore."

I was getting tired of being accused I was crazy. "Frankly Meatloaf, I don't give a bone what you think. You can go live at the pound."

The insult didn't seem to faze him.

"I been thinking about that. I don't think Robert will just dump us, I think he'll find us a new human if he moves to the city."

"So you don't care about that? You want a new human?"

"Taser, truth is, sometimes you just got to chill out and go with the flow."

"Don't give me that catcrap. Truth is, sometimes you gotta fight for what's right."

"Don't lecture me, pal, who was it came and pulled your bacon out of the fire?"

"You did, and I appreciate it. But we can't give up."

He lay his head back down. "Go eat some seed pods."

I didn't want mellow. I kept pacing and whining.

Henggggg. Hengggggggg.

Hush.

Henggggg. Hengggggggg.

Finally I got some help from an unlikely source.

Judy.

Robert, why don't you take them, maybe Taser has to pee.

He can pee in the backyard.

She seemed to chew on that, then offered another possibility.

Maybe he misses his friends.

Robert looked over at me. I was standing by the front door with the best pathetic dog-pout I could muster.

All right.

I did a little 360 spin just to let him know I was happy. It pays to reinforce good human behavior. He got some plastic poop bags from under the counter and walked toward the door.

Meatloaf, come on.

Meat didn't raise his head. He still looked stuck to the floor and didn't seem at all interested in exercise.

He's too tired, just take Taser, Judy said.

I can't help the fact I have more energy than Meatloaf, every dog is different. Besides, I was two years younger. Robert seemed OK with that too, he took me on the leash and we went out the door. By now it was mostly dark. That's no problem for me, I can see great in the dark, but Robert has those wimpy human eyes and they don't work very well after sundown. I walked just ahead to make sure it was safe for him.

When we got to the park it was empty. I was disappointed I'd missed everyone, I couldn't wait another day to see the pack. I had to see this thing through. Maybe I could—

Wait.

I saw Gizmo and his human at the far end of the park, they must have gotten here late, too. Gizmo was retrieving a thrown tennis ball. Robert called out to them, so they turned and came over to us. Robert started talking, it sounded like he was telling what happened with me and Meatloaf.

Gizmo looked happy to see me, but wondered about my partner.

"Where's Meatloaf?"

"He's too tired to come."

"We thought you were dead."

"Exaggerated rumors, as you can see." I gave him our story but I was hazy on the timing. I wasn't sure how long I'd been gone, it was all a blur.

"You're lucky to be alive. You ought to take it easy for a few days, let that wound heal so it doesn't get infected. You getting any antibiotics?"

"I guess, the vet gave me a shot at the pound. As far as resting, there's no time. I need the help of you and the rest of pack tomorrow. I can prove who murdered Vicki."

"Yeah? Who did it?"

"If you want to know, you have to come with me to Nelly's house. I'll show you then."

"Nelly's? We did that already. There's nothing there, Taser."

"We didn't look in the right place. Can you come by tomorrow? I need your help getting everyone over to help."

He didn't act happy about my request. "Look, I know you been through a lot, but the pack's still mad at you. I don't think anyone will help you with this."

I was confused. "I thought everyone wanted to solve this case. I thought we wanted to catch the murderer in our neighborhood."

Gizmo looked uncomfortable. "The pack, they think the police have the guy."

Now I understood. "They don't trust my judgment anymore."

"I'm sorry."

"That what Bandit thinks?"

"He and Remi."

"So now everyone thinks Bandit is brilliant?"

"Hey, I'm no fan of Bandit, trust me. But some of the others…" He trailed off.

"Simba?"

"He's been nosing around her, but she's resisting his advances."

At least someone was still loyal. I tried to convince Gizmo I was right this time.

"I admit I've been wrong about a few things, but if you look at all the evidence with me, you'll see I'm right. That's why I need everyone together."

213

"Here's the problem, Taser. I don't think they'll listen to you anymore."

"Oh. They think I'm as loony as Harley."

"Pretty much."

"That what you think?"

He looked at his paws. "You know, according to Meatloaf, Harley may not be loony."

"Your confidence is inspiring."

"Bandit's right about one thing. This coyote problem is a big deal to us small dogs. Look, you're a good fighter and they almost got you."

"There were two of them."

"But they're twice the size of us, I'm just a little squirt. And they're starving, desperate. They can just pick us up and cart us off."

"Buffy was an unusual case."

"Taser, face the facts. You're helping these coyotes and they still tried to kill you. They're bad news."

I was running out of arguments. "What about our humans? Our first job is to protect our humans."

"The police—"

"Have the wrong guy. I know, 'cause I saw the murder-human in back of our house the night of that big rain."

"How you know it was him? Anyone else see him? Like Meatloaf?"

"Harley saw him."

Gizmo scoffed. "There's a reliable source for you."

"Forget Harley, you think I'm lying to you? I thought you were my friend."

"I am your friend, Taser. But, I'm sorry, I can't help you anymore."

I was too surprised to answer. I stood there while he ran over to his human. In a moment, they were gone.

It was just me and Robert in the warm evening breeze.

***

When we got back to the house, Meatloaf was snoring. I went outside and wandered around, sniffing to see what had changed while I was gone. It smelled like the cat across the street had been all around our back yard. He'd even used our gravel for a toilet. Uggg. I was gonna get him for that insult.

And the rabbits had snuck in and eaten some of our purple lantana flowers. That just shows how important me and Meatloaf are around here. The place goes to the felines when we're gone.

I walked into the doghouse, it looked like my clues were still there. I sniffed the briefcase. Then I sniffed it again. The scent was as faint as ever, the problem was nobody else could smell it. Maybe it was time to get this thing open and look, maybe it would prove my theory to everyone.

But how?

There was only one way, I needed a human tool. I had to confront Robert with it. I considered the seriousness of my move, then I decided it was now or never. Tomorrow morning, first thing, I was gonna drag the briefcase in the house for Robert to find and open. The rest would be up to him.

THIRTY-FIVE

When morning came, I had the feeling it would be an important day. As soon as I heard the water running upstairs, I went out to get the briefcase. Meatloaf came out to see what I was doing.

"You're what?"

"He needs to see it."

"He'll know you went to Nelly's."

"No, he won't know where I got it."

I struggled to get it to the dog door, the effort made my wounded shoulder hurt. I didn't want to ask Meatloaf for help because I didn't want to get him in trouble. Luckily, our dog door was bigger than Nelly's so I didn't have much trouble getting it inside. I jumped through the door and dragged it to the foot of the stairs. Meatloaf hid in the kitchen while I lay down and started chewing on the handle like it was a big black leather bone I had found.

I kept one eye on the stairs while I pretended to chew.

Meatloaf peeked around the corner to see what was up, then he turned and went back in the kitchen. He wasn't happy. Finally Robert appeared at the top of the stairs. He was dressed up even nicer than a regular work day. He had on black pants and a black coat, with black shiny shoes.

Taser? What've you got?

He came down and picked up the briefcase. Apparently he didn't think I should be chewing it.

No!

I got up and moved to the living room to watch.

Robert looked closely at the outside of the briefcase, then he fumbled with the latch until he got it. He opened it up and peered inside, then he reached in and took out a plastic bag and some photos. When he looked at the photos his whole expression changed. His smell changed too, and it scared me. He opened the plastic bag and looked inside. He looked at a few more papers inside, then he put the plastic bag and the photos back in the briefcase.

He took the whole thing out to the garage and stuck it in the trunk of the Volvo. When he came back in he didn't talk to me or Meatloaf. Meat was still hiding in the kitchen waiting for me.

"What happened?" he asked.

I wasn't sure. "Nothing good. I've never seen him like this."

Robert went in the kitchen and sat down at the table. He didn't make a move to feed us, he didn't make any coffee, he didn't get the paper.

"See what you did?" said Meatloaf. "Now we won't get first meal."

"He's too upset, better just leave him alone."

We lay down in the corner and pretended we were invisible. We didn't want to get yelled at. I looked at his black clothes, then I understood.

"The funeral. Vicki's funeral is today," I said.

Meatloaf looked at Robert. "That's what they said, everyone wears black."

When Judy came downstairs, she was wearing black too, a black dress and black shiny shoes. Robert ignored her, and we didn't get up to greet her either. She got an envelope or card or something from the cabinet, then they both got in the car and drove off. The only sound I could hear was Meatloaf's stomach growling.

"How come they didn't feed us?" he asked.

"Because they were thinking of something else. I don't think Robert liked what he found in the briefcase."

"What was it?"

"Do you remember when we got locked in the garage for sniffing Judy's crotch."

"You mean when you sniffed Judy's crotch."

"I said it wasn't her normal odor."

"But what's in the briefcase?"

"That smell."

He cocked his head. "I don't follow."

"Come with me to Nelly's place and I'll show you."

Meatloaf started whining. "Noooooooooooooo. Not Nelly's. No. No. No."

"Meat. Snap out of it. Are you feline or canine? Come on."

He whined some more, but finally relented. We drank a bunch of water and went out to the side yard. I was a little worried my shoulder hurt too bad to jump up and unlatch the gate.

I shouldn't have worried. The gate was padlocked.

"What the?"

Meatloaf sat down. "That's what you get for breaking the rules. Now we're locked up for good. Nobody but Robert can open that gate now."

Catcrap.

The lock was shiny new, it looked like a combination lock. Meatloaf was right, probably only Robert knew the combination. I didn't know what to do, so I sat down too. It was impossible for us to get over the gate, we might have to wait for another day. Except...

"Hey Meat. Didn't the pack say everyone in the neighborhood was going to the funeral?"

"Yep."

"So we got to go today while no one is around. We gotta break out."

"Good luck."

"Come on, we can do it. How'd you get your idea for breakin' out?"

"Harley helped me. He warned me when Winston's humans walked by, then I got them to open the gate." He looked at the lock. "Even they couldn't open that now."

There wasn't time to dig out, besides, my shoulder hurt too bad. "Harley have any other ideas?"

"Wait for someone to open the front door and sneak out."

"No good. Anything else?"

Meatloaf scratched behind his ear. "He said if we could get in the garage, we could open the big door with the button."

I'd seen Robert do that, but the big door always scared me. It looked like it could squash us like a bug.

"Let's go look," I said.

We went in and trotted to the garage door, hoping it might be cracked open a bit. Nope. It was shut tighter than my butt at the Vets.

"No luck," said Meatloaf.

"Now wait a minute. We've seen them open these a million times. They just turn and push."

"Or pull."

"Right. We can do that. There's two of us, I'll turn and you push."

"Or pull," said Meatloaf.

"Yeah, yeah. Now wait."

I stood on my hind legs and bit into the door knob, then turned to the right.

"Huuhhh. Huuhhh."

"What'd you say?" asked Meatloaf

"Huuhhh. Huuhhh. Huuhhh."

"Do I want to dance?"

I let go of the knob. "Meat! Just push!"

"Now?"

"No! When I turn it."

I tried again.

"Huuhhh. Huuhhh."

Meatloaf pushed and the door opened, then we ran in the garage before the door swung shut. The garage seemed big and empty without any cars.

"Good work," I told Meatloaf. "Now what?"

"Harley said there's a button on the side of the door." He walked over to it. "Right here."

The button halfway up was small and black, it looked much too small to open such a big door.

"Go ahead, push it."

Meatloaf got on his hind legs and pushed. Nothing happened. Then he pushed again, the door jumped and started up. Immediately we ran out in the bright day-light, where we discovered a new surprise. Sitting and waiting on the driveway was Gizmo.

"Gizmo, you dog. You came to help."

"You didn't think I was gonna let you guys get all the glory, did you?"

I ran up to him and gave him a little push, I was so glad to see him. He pushed me back.

"OK, what do you want me to do?" he asked.

"Can you jump the fence at Nelly's house and get the gate open?"

"Is Lassie a sexy bitch? Let's go."

We ran across our neighbor's yards until we got to Nelly's. Gizmo barely slowed his run when he got to the house, he bounced off the wall, then onto and over the fence. Of course Harley barked pathetically, and Roxie showed up at her fence gate with questions.

"Hey guys. What are you up to?"

Gizmo had Nelly's gate open in time to walk out and answer her question. "We're solving the murder today."

She hesitated. "Well, can I help? I'd like to see what you're doing."

"Actually," I said, "I need everyone's help. We've got to confront the killer."

"It's not my human—is it?" Roxie asked.

"No, Roxie." I turned to Gizmo. "We need the whole pack over here. Even Harley."

"Harley?"

"He helped Meatloaf escape. We owe him a favor, and we can use his help today. There's a lot of work to do."

"What about Bandit?"

"Bandit and Remi can chew rocks, I don't want 'em here. They'll just sabotage the investigation."

Gizmo jumped over Roxie's fence. In a minute he had her out.

"It looks like all the humans are at the funeral," I said. "You won't have any trouble with our pack's masters."

"Who next?" asked Gizmo.

"Get Harley, then Winston and Simba. I'm gonna go inside and look around."

"I'll go with Gizmo," said Roxie. "We may have to convince them to come."

They ran off, leaving us in the back yard.

"I'm going inside," I said.

"I'll stand guard and bark if anyone shows up," said Meatloaf.

I went in the dog door of Nelly's house. The first thing I noticed was the smells were fainter, but now there were new odors. I smelled ham and beef, different sandwiches, sweet stuff and breads. It looked like party food for sure. The counters were piled with plastic plates and cups and paper napkins. I walked in the living room, everything was clean and nice. I didn't go down to the bedrooms, I didn't see what it would add and I didn't want to see the murder scene again. I noticed all the doors were closed, anyway.

Then I heard barking.

I went outside, afraid we were busted before we could begin. But Meatloaf was just standing there talkin' to Harley.

"It's Bandit," they said.

"Woof woof woof."

I jogged over to Bandit's side of the yard.

"Hey. Shut up over there, buttsniffer."

"What's happening?" Bandit yelled. "You guys can't just break in that house. I'm gonna bark for the police."

"Go ahead, loser. We're gonna need them."

Just then the pack arrived, so I ran over to the gate to greet them.

"Thanks for coming, everyone." I nodded at Simba. She smiled coyly but didn't say anything. She looked as good as ever.

"Everyone know Harley?"

They all did, but Roxie acted shy when she spoke to her next-door neighbor. "Wow. You're even bigger than your bark."

"That's me," Harley said. "Big, bad and black."

"All right," said Winston. "What the bloody hell is goin' on?"

"We're here to find the proof of who killed Nelly's female. Please, come in the backyard with me."

I led them to the rear and we stood in a little circle.

"Harley, you don't know everything, so we'll go over it again."

"That's cool."

"The night of the murder, Roxie was next door, she heard what happened. She heard the window glass breaking, she heard Nelly's howl. But before that she heard something else, she heard some scraping sounds."

"Scrapin' ?" asked Harley.

"Like something being dragged across the gravel," Roxie said.

"A body?"

"No."

"We don't know what it was," said Simba.

"I do." They all looked at me. I kept talking.

"Look at this little tree we're standing next to." Its leaves had fallen on the ground. "It's dead. The killer murdered this tree, too."

Winston looked at me impatiently. "Speak up, man. Who do you think it is?"

"Victor."

"Impossible. He was away on business."

"That's what he wanted everyone to think, it was his alibi. He left on business, but then he snuck back into town, walked thru the desert and came over the back fence to kill Vicki."

"That's crazy, there's no way to prove that," said Roxie.

"We can prove it. We have to dig up this dead tree. The murder weapon is buried underneath this tree."

The pack put their noses to the base of the tree and sniffed. They looked at me, then sniffed some more.

"I can't smell anything."

"Neither can I."

"Me either."

I asked the new member of our group. "Harley? What do you smell?"

"All I smell is manure, Jack."

"That's the point. Victor dumped a bunch of manure in there to cover the blood smell. Please, sit and listen." I waited until I had all their attention. "This how he did it. He dug the hole a couple days before, but he left the new tree off to the side in its container. Victor was always working in the yard, no one would see this as unusual. Then he went away on business, only to sneak back into town. He jumped the fence that night and went in the back door."

"Again, no way to prove that," said Roxie.

"Yes there is, by your own witness," I said. "You heard the glass break, then you heard Nelly howl a little later."

"That's true, I said that."

"But what you didn't hear was Nelly barking. Nelly didn't bark at the intruder because she knew him. It was her master who came in the back door."

"Of course."

"That's it."

"I say, that's a curious incident," said Winston. "The dog that didn't bark in the nightime. Where have I heard that before?"

No one knew, so I continued. "Victor comes in the house and murders Vicki, then he throws the murder weapon in the hole. He drags the tree over and drops it in, and then he fills the hole with dirt and manure. There's what's left of the fertilizer bag there." I pointed to the corner of the house.

"The tree hid the weapon and the manure hid the blood smell, but the hot fertilizer burned the tree and it died after a couple days. According to the friend I met in the pound—he's a landscaper's dog—manure will do that, especially in the hot-time."

"Victor was a great landscaper, so why would he make that mistake?"

"Because it was more important to hide the smell. Then after everything, Victor breaks the rear window so it looks like an intruder went in that way, then he hops the fence and gets away. He probably went back out of town."

"And then Nelly howled when she found Vicki."

"It's so sad," said Simba.

"It's all in the timing, no wonder we didn't get it at first," said Winston.

"Woof woof woof."

Everyone turned to look next door.

"That's just Bandit complaining about us trespassing. Ignore him," I said.

Simba looked worried. "Remember what my humans said. Victor is moving away after the funeral today, this is our last chance to catch him."

"Then I hope you're correct," said Winston.

Gizmo sniffed the ground. "You can smell something down there?"

I nodded. "I smell metal and I smell Vicki's blood. Somethin's under that tree."

"I don't smell any blood," said Winston.

Meatloaf stuck up for me. "Taser's got the best nose in town, we all know that. You gotta trust him."

"I say we dig down and look," said Simba. "I think he's right."

She beamed at me.

Harley pawed once at the earth. "It's still soft from the rain. I can do this no sweat."

He started digging quickly on one side, his big Rottweiler paws and claws scratching deep into the earth. The dirt flew so far it hit the fence. Gizmo and Meatloaf went to work on the other sides.

The rest of us watched from the sidelines. The tree wasn't as big as the others, so the digging went fast. Soon they were down a deeper distance than Gizmo was tall.

"Anything yet?" I asked.

"Nope."

Dirt and manure was piling up on all sides. I started to get nervous, what if I was wrong? Then I realized the reason it was taking so long.

"I'm afraid what we're lookin' for is gonna be on the bottom, guys."

They stopped to take a rest. The heat wasn't helping matters, I was sure everyone was as thirsty as me.

"Damn, Jack. I hope you got the right tree," said Harley. "We're halfway to Petworld."

Meatloaf lay down on the ground, panting. "I'm seriously out of shape."

"Oh, you gots a shape," said Harley. "A big fat one."

I moved closer to the hole. "Let me dig a while."

Gizmo stopped me from jumping in. "Not with that shoulder, you need to rest and keep it clean."

He hopped back in, then looked up at us. "I smell something," he said. "I think it's blood."

Now they all got back in the hole, even Roxie joined in. Pretty soon the dirt was flying again.

"Got something." Gizmo jumped out with a cloth glove in his mouth and dropped it at my feet. It was a gardening glove, but it looked and smelled like it had blood on it.

"I got somethin' too."

Harley pulled on something long, it was a sleeve from some clothes. He dug some more. We finally got it all out and spread it on the ground, it looked like a black jogging suit, a one-piece jogging suit with splotchy blood stains.

"Roxie," I said. "You know Victor's scent better than me, can you smell him on this?"

She put her nose to the suit. "It's definitely Victor's scent. And it has Vicki's blood on it."

They dug some more and Roxie found the other glove. Finally there wasn't enough dirt around the tree to support it. The dead tree trunk leaned to one side of the hole.

"Hey!" yelled Meatloaf. "I think I found the weapon."

He brought a long serrated kitchen knife out of the hole and dropped it in front of us for inspection. Everyone sniffed it.

"The police will have to give it a proper test," said Winston. "But this is the murder weapon, it passes my nose test."

"Mine, too."

"And mine."

"Well, that's it," I said. "We got him."

THIRTY-SIX

We dragged all the evidence to the front yard grass and spread it out. The jump suit, the gloves and the bloody knife were all carefully arranged so they could be seen when everyone returned from the funeral.

Then we lay down on the grass in the shade of Victor's two big trees. We took turns going inside to drink out of the toilet, and Harley and Meatloaf pulled down a bag of rolls and brought them out so we could have a little picnic while we were waiting. I don't know how long we'd been there, but it seemed like a long while. I was getting nervous they weren't coming, so I asked about it.

"So Roxie. How long is a funeral?"

She thought. "About as long as two Animal Channel shows. But then everyone drives to the cemetery for the burial. They'll all be here eventually, they all want to eat."

"Who could be hungry after burying a friend," Simba asked.

"I could," said Meatloaf. "Especially today, I didn't get first-meal."

"Eat another roll."

We waited some more, then all of a sudden a line of cars pulled up in front of the house. I recognized most from our neighborhood. Victor was in the first car, it hadn't stopped moving before he was yelling at us to get off his grass. Then he saw there were seven of us, all sprawled comfortably, some even eating his party food. He jumped out of the front seat, spitting mad and waving his arms.

Bad dogs! Get off my grass!

His yelling didn't bother any us, we didn't move an inch. We knew who the bad dog was. Then everyone else got out of their cars, I saw all the pack's humans, both male and female. They were all dressed in black and staring at us with wonder. Judy and Robert stood on the driveway, speechless also. The only one ranting was Victor, everyone else was looking at the dirt and blood-caked jogging suit. Then Victor saw what everyone was staring at, and he shut up and stared too.

Robert walked over and bent down to get a closer look at the clothes and the knife. He didn't touch anything, but he looked at me and Meatloaf funny. Then he stood up and spoke to the murderer.

Victor. Can you explain this?

Victor looked like a rat I cornered one time in my first house. The look was a mixture of panic, guilt and desperation. He hung his head and said nothing.

All of a sudden he broke away and started running down the street.

"He's getting away!" Simba yelled.

I got to my feet, but Harley was already moving. He leaped up and ran full speed after Victor, catching him only one house away. He stopped the killer in his tracks by clamping his huge jaws to his leg. Victor screamed in pain.

AUUUWWWWW!

Our humans were right behind Harley. Roxie's male and Harley's male grabbed Victor by the arms and dragged him back to the yard, Harley still attached to his leg. Finally he let go at his master's command.

I looked around for Robert, but he was off opening the trunk of Judy's car. He emerged with the black briefcase and confronted Victor with it. He pulled out the plastic bag and the photos and stuck both items in Victor's face. Then the yelling started. Victor took a swing at Robert but he backed away and swung himself. In a second it was a full-fledged fight. Robert connected with a blow to Victor's stomach and he doubled over.

"Cool," said Gizmo.

The briefcase and its contents fell on the sidewalk. I saw Winston hop up to look at the photos in spite of the fight, everyone else stayed put. I wasn't gonna get involved, I felt I'd done my work. Meatloaf nudged me from our shady spot on the lawn.

"Hey Taser. What's in that plastic bag?"

"Judy's black panties."

"Wow. Kinky," Meatloaf said. "I thought it was just me."

"The panties had the smell that confused me," I said. "I could pick it up faintly in the briefcase, but I knew it wasn't her normal smell. It turns out it was a mix of Judy and Victor."

"And that day we got thrown in the garage, when Judy came home from her trip?"

"She had that same smell."

We looked over at our Judy, she stood motionless, both her hands covering her face. I almost felt sorry for her.

The men tried to breakup the fight, but Robert was too mad to quit before he got in a few more blows. They finally all restrained Victor's hands with a leather belt and made him sit on the ground. Harley stood guard over him, growling quietly in his face. Whenever he moved, Harley bared his teeth. Everyone was impressed with Harley's ferocity, especially Roxie.

"Winston!" I called out and he ran over for my question.

"What's in those photographs?"

He hesitated. "It looks like Judy and Victor to me, but I've never seen them with their clothes off."

"And they're..."

He nodded. "Doggy-style. And then some."

"Well, I'll be a son of a bitch."

"Really?" Winston said. "I'm a bloody son of a bitch, too."

"Me too," said Meatloaf.

"Don't forget me."

"Those photographs," I said. "I wonder if they were in that camera?"

"What camera?"

"You remember when Vicki was murdered? The police said the only thing taken was a camera. Maybe these photos were from that camera."

"I bet Vicki found them," said Winston. "They had a row and she threatened to leave. That's why he killed her, before she divorced him and took all his money."

I wasn't sure about that. "Maybe. Or maybe he didn't like everyone coming over and mounting his mate while he was gone."

"Jealousy. That's the motive I told you first," said Winston.

The black and white police cars finally showed up, there were three of them. They put Robert in a backseat and then they looked at our dog evidence. They talked to Judy, too, and then they took her away. I felt bad for Robert but I wasn't sad to see her go.

She was a cold one. I always thought she would have been happier with a Siamese cat than with me and Meatloaf.

I saw a couple official-type humans in regular clothes starting to take pictures of everything. They spent some time in the backyard at the tree hole and then moved up front, photographing all the stuff we dug up. They talked like it was the scent that led us to find the bloody items. We let them believe it, in a sense they were right. I think Robert had other ideas. He kept looking over at us.

The photographer took our pictures next, first individually, then as a group. That's when I noticed we all weren't in the front yard anymore.

"Hey, where's Harley?" I asked.

"And Roxie?" asked Simba.

Everyone glanced around.

"I think they're sniffing bushes around the side of the house," said Winston. "I'll go get 'em. He ran off, then returned with a somber expression on his face.

"Ahhh, better not go over there."

"What's the problem?"

"It's...it's the hunchback beast with eight legs."

"Roxie? Oh my," said Simba.

230

I shrugged. No big deal.
Dogs will be dogs.
Sometimes.

EPILOGUE

Four months later

It was cold, even for Thanksgiving Day.

Me and Meatloaf were still panting from the hike as we stood next to Robert's new Jeep, waiting while he got some water for us. When he set down a bowl full we drank our fill and let the bright day-light warm us up.

A Thanksgiving hike was just what I needed to work up my appetite for the big meal. Meat complained that he didn't need any exercise to appreciate his turkey and mashed potato dinner, but he came along anyway. Our weekly hikes seemed to be helping his limp, or maybe it was because he'd lost some weight doing it. I knew they were doing me some good, my cuts and my shoulder were all healed up and I was stronger than ever.

The Valley air was crisp and clean from all the rain we'd been getting, I could see all the way to downtown Phoenix. I turned around and looked up at the McDowell Mountains, thinking Dominga and the other coyotes probably had good hunting up there now. They all seem to have migrated out of the neighborhood up to the hills after the rain and the wild game came back, it was pretty quiet on our streets these days.

We hopped in the shiny grey Jeep for our trip home. Traffic was light, I figured everyone must be home making dinner. I drooled a little thinking about the gravy we'd be getting. When I looked over at Meat, I saw he was droolin' too.

We drove in our subdivision and up the street toward our house. When we cruised past Simba's place, I looked but didn't see her. She was probably eating dinner. I'd wait and see her at the park next time, she kinda expected it since we were close now. At least since Bandit and his humans moved away, we didn't have to put up with his constant sniffing around us. I wasn't sad to see him go. Luckily, no other neighbors seemed interested in leaving, some had even hung Christmas lights already.

I only saw one flipper sign during our drive home through the neighborhood. Robert wasn't selling our house anymore. He said the housing boom died and home prices went in the toilet, so it wasn't a good time to sell, but I don't think he ever wanted too. Frankly, I was glad the neighborhood was settling in, I didn't want any of our pack movin' away.

The one sign still up was at Nelly's old house, it had been remodeled and fixed up with fresh paint inside and out. I hoped the new buyers owned a dog. Not that we could replace Nelly, we still missed her. Simba said she was doing fine, that she was living with Vicki's sister in Phoenix.

Robert pulled in our driveway and opened the big garage door. We ran in the house so we could inhale the dinner smells filling the warm kitchen. Robert peeked at the turkey in the oven and then set the table. He put his plate on our little kitchen table next to some candles, then he put a plate for me and one for Meatloaf right next to him on the floor. It was our own little feast. There were only three of us now, but we weren't lonely, we preferred it that way.

Robert said Gizmo and his humans were coming over later for dessert. That was cool. Robert didn't seem to miss Judy at all, and since all her clothes and stuff were gone, I doubted she was ever coming back. I heard about Victor and his conviction on the dinner news channel, but I'm not sure what happened to Judy. I hope he just gets another dog instead.

Finally Robert took the turkey out of the oven. He messed around at the stove a while, it looked like he was smashing the potatoes. When everything was ready and it was cool enough to eat, we said thanks for all our stuff. Then we all ate too much, and I have to say, it was the best meal I'd ever had.

Robert put a football game on the television after the meal and we all fell asleep, even him. It was pretty-much a perfect day.

When Gizmo brought his humans over later, they got to eat dessert but we only got to watch. No pumpkin pie for dogs, they said. Meatloaf mumbled something about specism, but everyone ignored him. It was his issue.

Later, after everyone had left, I went out back to walk off that full feeling. The brisk air woke up all my senses, and I thought I heard coyote howls off in the distance. I went inside to get Meatloaf up, he was planted solid by the burning fireplace.

"Hey Meat, come outside with me, it's great out back."

"No way, I'm too warm and cozy."

"I need your ears, I think I hear something interesting."

"That's your turkey digesting."

"Please."

He struggled to his feet and followed me outside, grumbling the whole time. When we got out to the patio we sat down and listened to the desert night. Sound traveled well in the crisp clear air. The howls rolled down the mountain right into our backyard--one strong howl mixed with two frail howls.

Yip Yip Oooooooooooooooo. ooooo. ooooo.

Meat looked over at me.

"It's Dominga. But I never heard the other two."

I hadn't either, until tonight.

"Those are her cubs. It looks like they survived the hot-time, it looks like they're gonna be all right now."

Meatloaf nodded. "I hope they got a Thanksgiving rabbit."

"I'm sure they did."

We listened a while, watching the stars.

"Hey Taze, you think she's talking to us?"

"Yeah, I do."

"What's she saying?"

I listened again. Her anger was gone, it sounded more like a joyful noise coming off the mountain.

"Partner, I think they're just happy to be alive."

Yip Yip Oooooooooooooooooooooooooooooooooooooooooooooo.

END

A PG version of Howl in the Night is available as
A HOWL AT MIDNIGHT
For Young Readers

Made in the USA
Lexington, KY
24 May 2012